FLUSH

KATE FLINT is Professor of English at Rutgers University, New Brunswick. She previously taught for fifteen years at the University of Oxford. A cultural historian and writer on the Victorians and the early twentieth century, her books include *The Victorians and the Visual Imagination* (OUP, 2000) and *The Woman Reader, 1837–1914* (OUP, 1993), both of which won the British Academy's Rose Mary Crawshay prize. She has edited and published articles on a number of works by Dickens and Virginia Woolf, among other authors, and written on subjects ranging from Pre-Raphaelitism to contemporary Black British fiction. She lives with three cats.

OXFORD WORLD'S CLASSICS

*For over 100 years Oxford World's Classics have brought
readers closer to the world's great literature. Now with over 700
titles—from the 4,000-year-old myths of Mesopotamia to the
twentieth century's greatest novels—the series makes available
lesser-known as well as celebrated writing.*

*The pocket-sized hardbacks of the early years contained
introductions by Virginia Woolf, T. S. Eliot, Graham Greene,
and other literary figures which enriched the experience of reading.
Today the series is recognized for its fine scholarship and
reliability in texts that span world literature, drama and poetry,
religion, philosophy and politics. Each edition includes perceptive
commentary and essential background information to meet the
changing needs of readers.*

OXFORD WORLD'S CLASSICS

VIRGINIA WOOLF

Flush

Edited with an Introduction and Notes by
KATE FLINT

OXFORD
UNIVERSITY PRESS

OXFORD

UNIVERSITY PRESS

Great Clarendon Street, Oxford OX2 6DP

Oxford University Press is a department of the University of Oxford.
It furthers the University's objective of excellence in research, scholarship,
and education by publishing worldwide in

Oxford New York

Auckland Bangkok Buenos Aires Cape Town Chennai
Dar es Salaam Delhi Hong Kong Istanbul Karachi Kolkata
Kuala Lumpur Madrid Melbourne Mexico City Mumbai Nairobi
São Paulo Shanghai Singapore Taipei Tokyo Toronto

Oxford is a registered trade mark of Oxford University Press
in the UK and in certain other countries

Published in the United States
by Oxford University Press Inc., New York

First published as an Oxford World's Classics paperback 1998
Reissued 2009

British Library Cataloguing in Publication Data

Data available

Library of Congress Cataloging in Publication Data
Woolf, Virginia, 1882–1941.
Flush/Virginia Woolf; edited with an introduction by Kate Flint.
1. Flush (Dog)—Fiction. 2. Browning, Elizabeth Barrett,
1806–1861—Fiction. 3. Human-animal relationships—England—
Fiction. 4. Women poets, English—19th century—Fiction. 5. Women
dog owners—England—Fiction. 6. Dogs—Fiction. I. Title.
PR6045.072F5 1998 823'.912—dc21 98–13090

ISBN 978–0–19–953929–1

15

Printed in Great Britain by
Clays Ltd, Elcograf S.p.A.

CONTENTS

ACKNOWLEDGEMENTS

I WOULD like to thank several people who have given me the opportunity to air my ideas about Woolf and animals in conferences and seminars, or who have given important help in other ways: Maria Teresa Chialant, Katherine Duncan-Jones, Carla Locatelli, and Oriana Palusci.

BIOGRAPHICAL PREFACE

VIRGINIA WOOLF was born Adeline Virginia Stephen on 25 January 1882 at 22 Hyde Park Gate, Kensington. Her father, Leslie Stephen, himself a widower, had married in 1878 Julia Jackson, widow of Herbert Duckworth. Between them they already had four children; a fifth, Vanessa, was born in 1879, a sixth, Thoby, in 1880. There followed Virginia and, in 1883, Adrian.

Both of the parents had strong family associations with literature. Leslie Stephen was the son of Sir James Stephen, a noted historian, and brother of Sir James Fitzjames Stephen, a distinguished lawyer and writer on law. His first wife was a daughter of Thackeray, his second had been an admired associate of the Pre-Raphaelites, and also, like her first husband, had aristocratic connections. Stephen himself is best remembered as the founding editor of the *Dictionary of National Biography*, and as an alpinist, but he was also a remarkable journalist, biographer, and historian of ideas; his *History of English Thought in the Eighteenth Century* (1876) is still of great value. No doubt our strongest idea of him derives from the character of Mr Ramsay in *To the Lighthouse*; for a less impressionistic portrait, which conveys a strong sense of his centrality in the intellectual life of the time, one can consult Noël Annan's *Leslie Stephen* (revised edition, 1984).

Virginia had the free run of her father's library, a better substitute for the public school and university education she was denied than most women of the time could aspire to; her brothers, of course, were sent to Clifton and Westminster.

[vii]

Her mother died in 1895, and in that year she had her first breakdown, possibly related in some way to the sexual molestation of which her half-brother George Duckworth is accused. By 1897 she was able to read again, and did so voraciously: 'Gracious, child, how you gobble', remarked her father, who, with a liberality and good sense at odds with the age in which they lived, allowed her to choose her reading freely. In other respects her relationship with her father was difficult; his deafness and melancholy, his excessive emotionalism, not helped by successive bereavements, all increased her nervousness.

Stephen fell ill in 1902 and died in 1904. Virginia suffered another breakdown, during which she heard the birds singing in Greek, a language in which she had acquired some competence. On her recovery she moved, with her brothers and sister, to a house in Gordon Square, Bloomsbury; there, and subsequently at several other nearby addresses, what eventually became famous as the Bloomsbury Group took shape.

Virginia had long considered herself a writer. It was in 1905 that she began to write for publication in the *Times Literary Supplement*. In her circle (more loosely drawn than is sometimes supposed) were many whose names are now half-forgotten, but some were or became famous: J. M. Keynes and E. M. Forster and Roger Fry; also Clive Bell, who married Vanessa, Lytton Strachey, who once proposed marriage to her, and Leonard Woolf. Despite much ill health in these years, she travelled a good deal, and had an interesting social life in London. She did a little adult-education teaching, worked for female suffrage, and shared the excitement of Roger Fry's Post-Impressionist Exhibition in 1910. In 1912, after another bout of illness, she married Leonard Woolf.

She was thirty, and had not yet published a book, though *The Voyage Out* was in preparation. It was accepted for publication by her half-brother Gerald Duckworth in 1913 (it appeared in 1915). She was often ill with depression and anorexia, and in 1913 attempted suicide. But after a bout of violent madness her health seemed to settle down, and in 1917 a printing press was installed at Hogarth House, Richmond, where she and her husband were living. The Hogarth Press, later an illustrious institution, but at first meant in part as therapy for Virginia, was now inaugurated. She began *Night and Day*, and finished it in 1918. It was published by Duckworth in 1919, the year in which the Woolfs bought Monk's House, Rodmell, for £700. There, in 1920, she began *Jacob's Room*, finished, and published by the Woolf's own Hogarth Press, in 1922. In the following year she began *Mrs Dalloway* (finished in 1924, published 1925), when she was already working on *To the Lighthouse* (finished and published, after intervals of illness, in 1927). *Orlando*, a fantastic 'biography' of a man–woman, and a tribute to Virginia's close friendship with Vita Sackville-West, was written quite rapidly over the winter of 1927–8, and published, with considerable success, in October. *The Waves* was written and rewritten in 1930 and 1931 (published in October of that year). She had already started on *Flush*, the story of Elizabeth Barrett Browning's pet dog—another success with the public—and in 1932 began work on what became *The Years*.

This brief account of her work during the first twenty years of her marriage is of course incomplete; she had also written and published many shorter works, as well as both series of *The Common Reader*, and *A Room of One's Own*. There have been accounts of the marriage very hostile to Leonard Woolf, but he can hardly be accused of cramping her talent or hindering the development of her career.

The Years proved an agonizingly difficult book to finish, and was completely rewritten at least twice. Her friend Roger Fry having died in 1934, she planned to write a biography, but illnesses in 1936 delayed the project; towards the end of that year she began instead the polemical *Three Guineas*, published in 1938. *The Years* had meanwhile appeared in 1937, by which time she was again at work on the Fry biography, and already sketching in her head the book that was to be *Between the Acts*. *Roger Fry* was published in the terrifying summer of 1940. By the autumn of that year many of the familiar Bloomsbury houses had been destroyed or badly damaged by bombs. Back at Monk's House, she worked on *Between the Acts*, and finished it in February 1941. Thereafter her mental condition deteriorated alarmingly, and on 28 March, unable to face another bout of insanity, she drowned herself in the River Ouse.

Her career as a writer of fiction covers the years 1912–41, thirty years distracted by intermittent serious illness as well as by the demands, which she regarded as very important, of family and friends, and by the need or desire to write literary criticism and social comment. Her industry was extra-ordinary—nine highly-wrought novels, two or three of them among the great masterpieces of the form in this century, along with all the other writings, including the copious journals and letters that have been edited and published in recent years. Firmly set though her life was in the 'Bloomsbury' context—the agnostic ethic transformed from that of her forebears, the influence of G. E. Moore and the Cambridge Apostles, the individual brilliance of J. M. Keynes,

Strachey, Forster, and the others—we have come more and more to value the distinctiveness of her talent, so that she seems more and more to stand free of any context that might be thought to limit her. None of that company—except, perhaps, T. S. Eliot, who was on the fringe of it—did more to establish the possibilities of literary innovation, or to demonstrate that such innovation must be brought about by minds familiar with the innovations of the past. This is true originality. It was Eliot who said of *Jacob's Room* that in that book she had freed herself from any compromise between the traditional novel and her original gift; it was the freedom he himself sought in *The Waste Land*, published in the same year, a freedom that was dependent upon one's knowing with intimacy that with which compromise must be avoided, so that the knowledge became part of the originality. In fact she had 'gobbled' her father's books to a higher purpose than he could have understood.

Frank Kermode

INTRODUCTION

Woolf and Animals

ANIMALS—real, imaginary, and metaphorical—were a constant presence in Virginia Woolf's life. The Stephen family, into which she was born, and then the Woolfs, always had at least one dog in their household. Her husband Leonard even owned a marmoset. One of Woolf's first published essays was an obituary of the Stephens' family dog Shag: more significantly, her first published piece of sustained polemic was an article in support of the anti-plumage campaign, which sought to ban the use of feathers from exotic and endangered birds in adorning fashionable women's hats.[1] The Stephen siblings called each other by animal nicknames, a habit which Virginia extended to her friends and which continued throughout adult life, producing an entire personal bestiary. Virginia was always Billy, or Goat, or Ape to her sister Vanessa; Goat to her brother Thoby. To Leonard, she was 'Mandrill' to his 'Mongoose'. Vanessa was sometimes Sheepdog or Marmot; more often Dolphin. Writing to her lifelong friend Violet Dickinson, she was 'Sparroy'; Emma Vaughan was 'Dearest Toad' (and again, Woolf was Goat to her). She addressed her friend and lover Vita Sackville-West as 'Dearest Creature', a term of

---

[1] See Reginald Abbott, 'Birds Don't Sing in Greek: Virginia Woolf and "The Plumage Bill"', in Carol J. Adams and Josephine Donovan (eds.), *Animals & Women: Feminist Theoretical Explorations* (Durham, NC: Duke University Press, 1995), 263–89.

endearment bridging the animal and the human worlds, and
as Towser, the sheepdog; she made herself furry and vulnerable in referring to herself as a little mole, a little squirrel.
'*Flush*', wrote Quentin Bell in the biography of his aunt, 'is not
so much a book by a dog lover as a book by someone who
would love to be a dog.'[2]

Virginia's and Vita's was a very doggy relationship. Vita
gave the Woolfs a puppy, Pinker, in 1926, who became the
model for Flush when in 1932 Virginia came to write her
biography of Elizabeth Barrett Browning's spaniel of this
name. At around the same time that Vita sent Woolf a
photograph of her dogs, including Pinker ('may I keep it and
perhaps use it in my story?'),[3] Virginia half-heartedly
encouraged her to sell the manuscript of *Orlando* to an
American bidder: 'I will write another book and give you the
MS. instead—about turning into a rusty, clotted, hairy
faithful blue-eyed sheepdog.'[4] At times, Woolf would use her
habit of animalizing to merge with her creations: writing to
David Garnett, thanking him for his 'generous and wholly
delightful' review of *Flush* in the *New Statesman* (6 October
1933), she signed herself 'Yours affectionate old English
springer spaniel Virginia'.[5] It was a constant habit of Woolf's
mind to find animal correspondences for those whom she met:
Freud has 'a monkeys light eyes'; Roger Fry's sister Margery
is a 'yak'; Auden a 'small rough haired terrier man'; Aldous

[2] Quentin Bell, *Virginia Woolf: A Biography* (2 vols., London, The Hogarth Press, 1972), ii. 175.

[3] Virginia Woolf to Vita Sackville-West, 17 March 1932, *The Letters of Virginia Woolf*, ed. Nigel Nicolson and Joanne Trautmann (6 vols., London: Hogarth Press, 1975–84), v. 35.

[4] Virginia Woolf to Vita Sackville-West, 1 April 1932, ibid. 41.

[5] Virginia Woolf to David Garnett, 8 October 1933, ibid. 232.

Huxley a 'gigantic grasshopper'.[6] The same processes readily occur in her fictions: in *Mrs Dalloway* Elizabeth is to some a 'fawn', to others a 'long-legged colt'; Lady Bradshaw, wife of the appalling psychiatrist, appears at Clarissa's party 'in grey and silver, balancing like a sea-lion at the edge of its tank, barking for invitations, Duchesses, the typical successful man's wife';[7] in *To the Lighthouse*, the bereaved, desperate-looking Mr Ramsay ranges about 'like a lion seeking whom he could devour'.[8]

This drive towards animalization, the compulsive manufacturing of menageries both in Woolf's private language and in the rhetoric of her fictions, is an important part of the context in which one needs to examine Woolf's apparently light-hearted biography of a spaniel. *Flush* is a work which has received notoriously little critical attention. Response to it has too often taken Woolf's description of it as a 'joke' at face value, passing over it also, one might suspect, because of potential embarrassment at the doggy whimsy it undoubtedly contains. *Orlando*'s (1928) claim as a text which debunks patriarchal biographical styles, which interrogates the conventions of writing history, writing lives, has been taken far more seriously. As Sandra Gilbert has reminded us, Woolf's father, Leslie Stephen, had become the first editor of the prestigious *Dictionary of National Biography* in the year she was born, so she had been preoccupied with the personal but

---

[6] *The Diary of Virginia Woolf*, ed. Anne Olivier Bell, assisted by Andrew McNeillie (5 vols, London: The Hogarth Press, 1977–84): 29 January 1939, v. 202; 18 April 1932, iv. 89; 25 June 1937, v. 98; 1 July 1926, iii. 93.

[7] Virginia Woolf, *Mrs Dalloway* (1925; Oxford: Oxford University Press, 1992), 239. Subsequent page references in parentheses in the text.

[8] Virginia Woolf, *To the Lighthouse* (1927; Oxford: Oxford University Press, 1992), 211. Subsequent page references in parentheses in the text.

often "official" genre of biography and its relationship to "official" public historiography from early in her career'.[9] *Orlando*'s ludic treatment of gender, its questioning of the relationship between appearance and interiority, its investigation of the human tendency to judge by appearances, its consideration of the negotiations which necessarily take place between individual sensibilities and what one might broadly see as the spirit of an age, its dominant tastes and prejudices and social customs, has ensured that it has been read as an important feminist work, pioneering in its form as well as in the issues it raises. But *Flush* also has a claim on our attention as a work which is simultaneously entertaining and serious. It, too, raises questions about gender and society, about freedom and control, about perception and expression. And in all of this, its relation to the far wider patterns of references to the animal world which thread through Woolf's works is of crucial importance.

Flush

Throughout her career, Woolf invokes the animal world both directly and metaphorically. Sometimes, she does so in order to express anger, or passion, or violence: elemental responses which exist across species. Sometimes, and this is particularly true in her private writings, she seems to find it easier to express intimate feelings through displacing them from the human sphere onto a cosier animal one. Most interestingly, however, she uses the presumed, customary split between the

[9] Sandra M. Gilbert, '*Orlando*', in Julia Briggs (ed.), *Virginia Woolf: Introductions to the Major Works* (London: Virago, 1994), 197.

animal and the human spheres in order to examine the way assumed hierarchies function within society. Frequently, this enables her to make cutting observations about injustices and inequalities in her society, and in the social structures which fed into many of the assumptions still current in her own time. The text in which she does this consistently, deliberately, is *Flush*.

Woolf started to write this biography of Elizabeth Barrett Browning's spaniel just after she finished *The Waves*, and envisaged it, like any biography, working as a sort of counterpoint to her fiction: the former allowed her to 'use her powers of representation reality accuracy; & to use my novels simply to express the general, the poetic'.[10] Partly, too, its writing was an economic gesture, or at least could be explained, defensively, as such: hoping by composing this apparently light-hearted text 'to stem the ruin we shall suffer from the failure of The Waves'.[11] She wrote to Lady Ottoline Morrell on 23 February 1933: 'I was so tired after the Waves, that I lay in the garden and read the Browning love letters, and the figure of their dog made me laugh so I couldn't resist making him a Life. I wanted to play a joke on Lytton—it was to parody him'[12]—parodying, in other words, Lytton Strachey's extravagant debunking of Victorian hypocrisy in *Eminent Victorians*, and tacitly restating, in the process, some of the reasons why the Victorian period, with its legacy of gender attitudes persisting into the present day, still deserved serious scrutiny.[13] For *Flush* is nowhere near as generically cut and

[10] Virginia Woolf, *Diary*, iv. 40.

[11] Virginia Woolf to Vita Sackville-West, 16 September 1931, *Letters*, iv. 380.

[12] Virginia Woolf to Lady Ottoline Morrell, 23 February 1933, ibid., v. 161–2.

[13] Necessarily, after the death of Lytton Strachey on 22 January 1932, something of the sense that Woolf was engaging in a playful dialogue with him was lost.

dried as her description to Lady Ottoline might suggest: rather it is, primarily, an allegory: a vehicle through which Woolf can investigate the position of the subordinate, seeing things—literally—from a low position. She acknowledges in a letter of 13 October 1933 that 'Yes, they are much alike, Mrs Browning and her dog',[14] and, stretching the work's potential implications further, writes to Lady Colefax on 22 October that 'it was all a matter of hints and shades, and practically no one has seen what I was after'.[15] To write the biography of a dog is without doubt to stretch the limits of literary canonicity.[16] Pamela Caughie has suggested that we should consider making a parallel between the woman writer's dog and the woman writer's servant, too, and notes that a six-page note on Wilson points us in that direction: Wilson, Woolf writes, 'was typical of the great army of her kind—the inscrutable, the all-but-silent, the all-but-invisible servant maids of history' (p. 113). Such a hint has, in its turn, been taken up by Margaret Forster in composing another fictional biography, *Lady's Maid* (1990), about this very woman. 'Flush's life', Caughie remarks, 'may not stand in for the lives of women we (propertied middle- and upper-class women) know; rather, *Flush* may stand as a testimony to the lives that have never been narrated, the inscrutable and therefore unrepresentable, the discarded and therefore wasted.'[17] But one should remember that Victorian women poets did not, in the 1930s, occupy the relatively prominent position they do now. 'Fate

[14] Virginia Woolf to Gladys Mulock, 13 October 1933, ibid. 234.

[15] Virginia Woolf to Sibyl Colefax, ?22 October 1933, ibid. 236.

[16] This point is well made in Pamela L. Caughie, '*Flush* and the Literary Canon: Oh where oh where has that little dog gone?', *Tulsa Studies in Women's Literature*, 10 (1991), 47–66.

[17] Ibid. 61.

has not been kind to Mrs Browning as a writer,' Woolf wrote in her essay on *Aurora Leigh*, published in the *Yale Review* in June 1931. 'Nobody reads her, nobody discusses her.'[18]

Flush is structured like a human biography, from birth through to death. The book traces the life of the spaniel from his country origins, his puppyhood spent with the writer Mary Mitford and her impecunious father, through his very sheltered existence in Wimpole Street with Elizabeth Barrett in her sick room. Opening with a solemn discussion of Flush's pedigree, the conventional importance paid to human genealogy in placing an individual within the class system, establishing their background, is both acknowledged and gently mocked. These introductory pages are part of a broader double-edged strategy on Woolf's part, whereby she both legitimizes her own biographic enterprise through footnotes and a list of sources, as though she were writing the life of a human subject, and makes her reader recognize the conventions of biography *as* conventions, through questioning their appropriateness when applied to a canine.

The events that matter in this biography are those that Woolf imagined making an impression on a dog's life, a further reminder that a shift of focus away from the well-known story of Elizabeth Barrett and Robert Browning might lead to less familiar elements of Victorian society coming to the fore. We learn of the terrors of his kidnapping by a gang of dog-stealers (which actually happened three times, but is here compressed, for dramatic resonance, into one episode). This traumatic time for Flush allowed Woolf to experiment with

---

[18] Virginia Woolf, 'Aurora Leigh', in *Collected Essays*, ed. Leonard Woolf (4 vols., London: Chatto and Windus, 1967), i. 209.

writing about slum life, a marked shift in her normal choice of London locations. Flush accompanies his mistress when she elopes to Italy with Robert Browning, both dog and woman finding a new freedom there. He travels with her back to England on vacation, and back again to Italy. He demonstrates a healthy scepticism towards his mistress's sudden fascination with the spirit world and table-rapping. In all of this, Woolf imagines what it may be like to apprehend the world from a different alignment of the senses, scent dominant over sight: in Italy Flush 'devoured whole bunches of ripe grapes largely because of their purple smell; he chewed and spat out whatever tough relic of goat or macaroni the Italian housewife had thrown from the balcony—goat and macaroni were raucous smells, crimson smells' (p. 87). He feels folds of drapery, marble, cobbled streets under his tongue and paws. And Woolf fantasizes about the freedom from the tyranny of words which makes the dog's sensual and emotional comprehension the more direct: 'In short, he knew Florence as no human being has ever known it; as Ruskin never knew it or George Eliot either. He knew it as only the dumb know. Not a single one of his myriad sensations ever submitted itself to the deformity of words' (p. 87). This final liberation is used to tie him in still further with Elizabeth Barrett Browning, since much earlier, Woolf used her weary words to R. H. Horne, describing how she was always 'Writing, writing, writing' (p. 27) to speculate: 'After all, she may have thought, do words say everything? Can words say anything? Do not words destroy the symbol that lies beyond the reach of words?' (p. 27).

Yet she makes it clear that Flush, after all, was not 'fated to remain for ever in a Paradise where essences exist in their utmost purity, and the naked soul of things presses on the naked nerve' (p. 88), for he has, in fact, come to live too close to humans, his life too closely blended with theirs, for her not to imagine that he felt frustration as well as bliss, a frustration of imperfect communication: he had 'lain upon human knees and heard men's voices. His flesh was veined with human passions; he knew all grades of jealousy, anger and despair' (p. 88). If on the one hand this is one of the book's many moments of anthropomorphism, it is also the Romantic version of what it is to have a poet's sensibility without the gift of expression; having what Wordsworth, in *The Excursion*, called 'the vision and the faculty divine; | Yet wanting the accomplishment of verse'.[19]

In Flush's old age, the parallel between dog and human grows ever closer: 'Her face with its wide mouth and its great eyes and its heavy curls was still oddly like his' (p. 105). The long-faced portrait of Elizabeth Barrett Browning with which Woolf illustrated her text, hair hanging in long loose locks like spaniel ears, brings home the point. 'Broken asunder, yet made in the same mould, could it be that each, perhaps, completed what was dormant in the other? But . . . She was woman; he was dog' (pp. 18–19). Whilst in practical terms this taxonomic splitting might be a barrier to marriage or sex between these complementary partners, the closeness between species is the assumption on which the book pivots. Thus the country dog finds himself needing to learn submission, to accept the authority of asphalt paths and men in shiny top hats and the demand that dogs be led on chains when taken for a walk in Regent's Park, a parallel to women's

---

[19] William Wordsworth, *The Excursion* (1814), i. 78–9.

internalization of the obligation to subjugate themselves to the confining social laws of patriarchy. In the invalid's bedroom, he learns to accept restraint: 'To resign, to control, to suppress the most violent instincts of his nature—that was the prime lesson of the bedroom school . . . Upon such a dog the atmosphere of the bedroom told with peculiar force. We cannot blame him if his sensibility was cultivated rather to the detriment of his sterner qualities' (pp. 25, 32). When he is kidnapped, his confinement in Whitechapel, despite the sordid nature of his surroundings, raises emotions in him which further parallel Elizabeth Barrett Browning's imprisonment in Wimpole Street: moreover, as Susan Squier has shown, the episode makes a point about the interaction of hierarchies in the organization of Victorian London life. The two locations are linked, as she says, by 'mutual economic dependence'.[20] Moreover, we are faced with the fact that if for Elizabeth Barrett, Flush was a love object, a person in his own right (his loss 'affected her as the loss of a child might have affected another woman',[21] Woolf writes in her essay on

[20] Susan Squier, *Virginia Woolf and London: The Sexual Politics of the City* (Chapel Hill, NC: University of North Carolina Press, 1985), 127. Squier, one of the very few critics to have taken this work seriously, makes a number of interesting points in her chapter on *Flush*, including drawing a comparison between Woolf's treatment of the kidnapping and the Jack the Ripper murders: 'Woolf's parallel phrasing and choice of details remarkably similar to those of the Ripper murder case imply that the link between the two seemingly diametrically opposed London environments—Wimpole Street and Whitechapel—was misogyny and sexual oppression. The novel anticipates contemporary feminist understanding of rape and pornography, presenting the kidnapping of Flush (and, by implication, the Ripper murders) as but a special instance of a general situation: the domination and oppression of women and other marginalized groups within patriarchal culture. Flush's kidnapping and imprisonment, with its horrible motif of the threatened package of his head and paws, implicitly recalls the murders of Jack the Ripper' (ibid. 132).

[21] Virginia Woolf, 'Aurora Leigh', 214.

Aurora Leigh), for another set of people, he was an object of economic exchange: valuable for his breeding, his pedigree, and because emotional worth could be turned into a site of blackmail.

The kidnapping of Flush is also used by Woolf to complicate that most prevalent of myths surrounding the Barretts of Wimpole Street: that Robert Browning was, unequivocally, a liberator, rescuing the poet from her tyrannical father, just as Elizabeth Barrett liberates Flush. For Browning is presented as less than enthusiastic about paying the ransom that is asked for the dog, reasoning that to capitulate to his captors' demands is to foster crime. In doing so, he is siding with Mr Barrett, siding with male logicality, male values. 'So, if she went to Whitechapel', Barrett meditates, 'she was siding against Robert Browning, and in favour of fathers, brothers and domineerers in general' (p. 62). In other words, there is no escaping the capturing nets of masculinity in this society, but an individual woman was faced with a number of circumscribed choices in which the actions to which she committed herself added up to an assertion of her own values. In these terms, rescuing Flush was as significant as eloping with Robert Browning. And it is notable that in tacitly dramatizing this point, Woolf, as the notes to this section of the text show, was highly selective in her evidence, omitting those portions of Robert Browning's letters which show him to have been making his most apparently unfeeling remarks in the mistaken belief that Flush, once located, would instantly be safely back at his mistress's side.

Class, like gender, is explored by Woolf in *Flush*, and in a way which heightens its connection with questions of national identity as well. In class terms, Flush accepts the privilege of rank—for in Victorian London snobbery is as rife in the world of pets as in that of humans. Harriet Ritvo notes in *The Animal Estate*, her fascinating study of the English and other creatures in the Victorian period, that the 'elaborately distinguished and carefully graduated classes' of the dog-breeding world 'mirrored breeders' desire to improve their own social positions ... [Their] goal was to celebrate their desire and ability to manipulate, rather than to produce animals that could be measured by such extrinsic standards as utility, beauty, or vigor'.[22] England was dominated by hierarchization, categorization, by regularization, by claustrophobia. These are figured in a dog's sensory consciousness by 'The confinement, the crowd of little objects, the blackbeetles by night, the bluebottles by day, the lingering odours of mutton, the perpetual presence on the sideboard of bananas' (p. 92), these last fruits tacitly signifying the whole reach of Empire that lay beyond the stuffy drawing-room, yet the expansion of which was symbiotically linked to the smugly ordered social stratification, with its genealogical gradations, against which Flush rebelled. By contrast, in Pisa, the spaniel 'faced the curious and at first upsetting truth that the laws of the Kennel Club are not universal' (p. 77); here 'though dogs abounded, there were no ranks; all—could it be possible?—were mongrels' (p. 74). His mental and indeed physical liberation in Italy goes in tandem with Elizabeth Barrett Browning's new found freedom, no longer treated as a delicate invalid: 'Here in Italy was freedom and life ... She was always comparing Pisa with London and saying how much she

---

[22] Harriet Ritvo, *The Animal Estate: The English and Other Creatures in the Victorian Age* (1987; London: Penguin Books, 1990), 115.

preferred Pisa. In the streets of Pisa pretty women could walk alone', unlike in 'poor, dull, damp, sunless, joyless, expensive, conventional England' (p. 76).

Flush is not without a capacity to irritate in its whimsicality, belonging, as it does, to a Victorian tradition of anthropomorphization. Woolf's own friends were somewhat divided in how to read it. So were the critics. Geoffrey Grigson, reviewing it in the *Morning Post*, complained that 'Its continual mock-heroic tone, its bantering pedantry, its agile verbosity make it the most tiresome book which Mrs Woolf has yet written'.[23] As condescending was the language used, even if with praise in mind, by Rose Macaulay in the *Spectator*, when she termed it a 'book of irresistible grace and charm'.[24] Woolf had worried that the book would seem over-feminine, that she would be dismissed as 'a ladylike prattler' for having written it: 'I shall very much dislike the popular success of Flush.'[25] She herself, with a hint of embarrassment, calls it a 'silly book';[26] she refers to the spaniel as an 'abominable dog'.[27] Its literary legacy was picked up when the *Times Literary Supplement* headlined its review 'Brown Beauty',[28] with a glance back to Anna Sewell's famous work *Black Beauty* (1877) which protested against ill-treatment of working horses. Yet *Black Beauty* is also significant for its wider role in demonstrating the involvement of women, in the later decades of the nineteenth century, in agitation for animal rights: campaigning against cruelty, against experimentation

[23] *Morning Post* (6 October 1933).
[24] Rose Macaulay, *Spectator*, 151 (6 October 1933), 450.
[25] Virginia Woolf, 2 October 1933, *Diary*, iv. 181.
[26] Virginia Woolf, 29 April 1933, ibid. 153.
[27] Virginia Woolf, 3 January 1933, ibid. 139.
[28] Unsigned review, 'Brown Beauty', *Times Literary Supplement* (5 Oct 1933), 667.

and vivisection. As Lynda Birke puts it in her article 'Exploring the Boundaries: Feminism, Animals, and Science', 'For these feminists, there were clear parallels in the ways that women and animals were treated by science.'[29] The ramifications of this broadbased humanitarianism fan out into still wider questions of rights. The moral philosopher Mary Midgley, in *Animals and Why They Matter*, draws attention to what she calls 'four distinct problems . . . the position of women, of slaves, of other races, and of non-human animals'—an alert reading of *Flush* suggests that we might add class position to this list. Midgley argues that they may be considered together, 'not because their logic is necessarily similar, but because their history is so'. She continues: 'Inspected calmly and without passion', the positions she enumerated 'might look very different. What unites them is that they scarcely ever are so inspected.'[30]

Humans and Animals

Woolf's sustained employment of references to animals may be considered through three linked propositions or sets of propositions. First, one can see that Woolf consciously invokes and then collapses traditional human–animal hierarchies in order to comment on social injustice, particularly concerning the position of women. This is applicable both to her own period and to her treatment of the Victorian society which preceded it. The homogenization of categories

[29] Lynda Birke, 'Exploring the Boundaries: Feminism, Animals, and Science', in Adams and Donovan (eds.), *Animals & Women*, 34.

[30] Mary Midgley, *Animals and Why They Matter* (Athens, Ga.: University of Georgia Press, 1984), 74.

in her comment in *A Room of One's Own* that women 'are, perhaps, the most discussed animal in the universe' is surely far from accidental.[31] In bringing humans and animals together, Woolf can be seen as part of a wider movement. Midgley has shown how, until recent times, humans and animals have been seen as quite separate within Western thought: 'the main official Christian doctrine has simply excluded animals from consideration as not having souls',[32] whilst Enlightenment thought, with its exaltation of reason, tended to arrive at the position that 'If animals are irrational, and value and dignity depend entirely on reason, animals cannot matter'.[33] But from the late eighteenth century onwards, laws started to be passed against the more extreme forms of cruelty against animals, customs started to change, and the permissible treatment of animals was brought within much narrower limits. Along with this went an increasing awareness that

human life really does have an animal basis—an emotional structure on which we build what is distinctively human. In spite of the differences, quite complex aspects of things like loneliness and play and maternal affection, ambition and rivalry and fear, turn out to be shared with other social creatures.[34]

And necessarily Darwin's work, particularly *On the Origin of Species*, helped to break down the human–animal divide not just through the general lines of its argument, but, as Gillian Beer has shown, through its language, its metaphoric resonances. In this text 'animals, plants, fishes, insects—the whole

[31] Virginia Woolf, *A Room of One's Own* (1929; Oxford: Oxford University Press, 1992), 34.
[32] Midgley, *Animals and Why They Matter*, 10.
[33] Ibid. 11.   [34] Ibid. 14.

of animate nature—become one moving and proliferating family. Words like "parent" and "birthplace", so often reserved for humankind, are . . . set at the service of all living forms.'[35] None the less, despite this linguistic as well as—in hypothetical terms—scientific bringing together as species, one must not forget that 'Real women and real animals', as Donna Haraway has put it, 'cannot escape their complex relations to the signifying systems and histories of domination that constructed Woman, the Primitive, Race, Nature, Animal, the Other to Man.'[36]

This leads into a second point: the fact that Woolf's capacity to break down the borderlines between human and animal raises a whole wider set of questions about rights. Woolf emerges, here, in a more complicated light, since at the time that she is critiquing certain aspects of her society, we can see that some of her thought is informed by apparently unconsciously held ideological assumptions. Although many of her ideas point forwards to debates about species diversity which are taking place today, in her earlier writings, at least, Woolf is not immune from a particular strand of Victorian thinking; that is, the parallelism between a desire to classify and control and put in zoos, and indeed to hunt and master, exotic animals, and the colonial policies adopted in the lands inhabited by these creatures. To take just one apparently casual reference on her part: in 1917 she notes in her diary the

[35] Gillian Beer, '"The Face of Nature": Anthropomorphic Elements in the Language of *The Origin of Species*', in Ludmilla Jordanova (ed.), *Languages of Nature: Critical Essays on Science and Literature* (London: Free Association Books, 1986), 223–4.

[36] Donna Haraway, 'Monkeys, Aliens, and Women: Love, Science, and Politics at the Intersection of Feminist Theory and Colonial Discourse', *Women's Studies International Forum*, 12/3 (1989), 295–312, at 296.

visit of E. W. Perera, an advocate from Ceylon, a 'poor little mahogany coloured wretch' with no variety of conversational subjects: 'The character of the Governor, & the sins of the Colonial Office, these are his topics; always the same stories, the same point of view, the same likeness to a caged monkey, suave on the surface, inscrutable beyond.'[37] He is belittled both by the animal reference and through ethnic stereotyping. This remark helps one identify something of a paradox in Woolf's use of animal imagery. For although she invokes the animal world as a means of claiming freedom—as we see in her frequent use of the image of the fish moving lithely through water, round rocky barriers, nosing against weeds, seeking out 'the pools, the depths, the dark places'[38] to describe the flexible movement of the imagination—this world of wild, as opposed to domestic, animals is frequently connected in the logic of her mind to the primeval, to the jungle, to the swamp. When, for example, Flush returns to Elizabeth Barrett's bedroom after being kidnapped: 'This room was no longer the whole world; it was only a shelter. It was only a dell arched over by one trembling dock-leaf in a forest where wild beasts prowled and venomous snakes coiled; where behind every tree lurked a murderer ready to pounce' (p. 67). Increasingly, in Woolf's writing, some animals are associated with the same kind of ruthless, mindless cruelty that characterizes Fascist brutality, patriarchal thoughtless cruelty. How, we will need to ask, is Woolf's concept of civilization, and the political questions of social hierarchies

[37] Virginia Woolf, 16 October 1917, *Diary*, i. 60–1.

[38] Virginia Woolf, 'Professions for Women' (delivered 1931; revised version published in *The Death of the Moth* 1942), in *Virginia Woolf: Women & Writing*, ed. and introd. Michèle Barrett (London: The Women's Press, 1979), 61.

that such a term raises, connected with her employment of animal terminology? If humans are like animals—and she continually suggests that they are—what does this say about the 'natural' when it comes to understanding human and social behaviour?

Woolf's assumption of the closeness between animals and humans leads to a third observation. One finds that to employ the register of the animal world allows Woolf to say things that she found difficult or impossible to address more directly. This is particularly true of the language of emotions, especially sexual feelings. This can be seen well in her figuring of Mrs Flanders in *Jacob's Room*. Mrs Flanders turns down a proposal of marriage from Mr Floyd, thinking, in what seems an inconsequential train of reasoning, that she had always disliked red hair in men. When Mr Floyd moves away, her youngest son chooses his ginger kitten to remember him by: the kitten's fur forms an analogy to Mr Floyd's own red pelt. In a narrative flashforward, we see Mrs Flanders stroking the kitten, now a very old and slightly mangy cat: '"Poor old Topaz," said Mrs Flanders, as he stretched himself out in the sun, and she smiled, thinking how she had had him gelded, and how she did not like red hair in men. Smiling, she went into the kitchen':[39] the nature of the smile is left hovering in the air. Is it a smile of displaced female triumph, with Mrs Flanders enjoying her imagined role as castrating victrix? or the recollection of a moment in the past that had been successfully negotiated? or a less definable expression of her delight in her own current domestic security, uninterrupted

[39] Virginia Woolf, *Jacob's Room* (1922; Oxford: Oxford University Press, 1992), 25. Subsequent page references in parentheses in the text.

by male sexual demands? For Woolf in her own life, the
natural world could provide her with images through which to
represent the intensity and, by inference, the danger of desire,
a knowledge of this intensity which rarely surfaces otherwise
even in her most private writings. Thus in her diary for 13
June 1932 she records that the bees swarmed: 'Bees shoot
whizz, like arrows of desire: fierce, sexual; weave cats cradles
in the air; each whizzing from string; the whole air full of
vibration: of beauty, of this burning arrowy desire; & speed: I
still think the quivering shifting bee bag [the bag in which the
swarm was gathered] the most sexual & sensual symbol.'[40] On
other occasions, her own body seems possessed by the animal,
something which is both part of her and seen as strange, other.
Tired after finishing *The Waves*, and putting together the
second volume of her essays, *The Common Reader*, she writes
of fainting: 'That is the galloping horses got wild in my
head . . . the pulse leapt into my head & beat & beat, more
savagely, more quickly. I am going to faint I said & slipped off
my chair & lay on the grass. Oh no I was not unconscious. I
was alive; but possessed with this struggling team in my head:
galloping, pounding. I thought something will burst in my
brain if this goes on.'[41] It is as if Woolf has to cut across the
habitual dividing-line between human and animal to talk of
extremes, of boundaries of experience, or, in the case of Mrs
Flanders, of the uncertain borderline of conscious and unconscious.

The question of animals and intimacy is deeply relevant to
Flush. Woolf's narrative stresses the bond between the poet

[40] Virginia Woolf, 13 June 1932, *Diary*, iv. 109.
[41] Woolf, 17 August 1932, ibid. 121.

and her pet: '"He is worth loving, is he not?" she asked of Mr Horne. And whatever answer Mr Horne might give, Miss Barrett was positive of her own. She loved Flush, and Flush was worthy of her love' (p. 33). If anything, Woolf is sparing in the number of direct quotations which she gives from Elizabeth Barrett's letters—particularly her letters to Mary Mitford, who initially gave the spaniel puppy to her—which show the amount of emotional investment, the loving attention, which Barrett bestowed upon her animal companion. These letters reveal the degree to which he was a focus, an outlet for those capacities for love which were to show themselves in her courtship with Robert Browning. This courtship is, in Woolf's work, continually presented from Flush's point of view: 'It was not merely that Miss Barrett was changing towards Mr Browning—she was changing in every relation—in her feeling towards Flush himself. She treated his advances more brusquely; she cut short his endearments laughingly; she made him feel that there was something petty, silly, affected, in his old affectionate ways. His vanity was exacerbated. His jealousy was inflamed' (p. 42). It is the dog's loss that we are made to feel, rather than his person's gain.

In her own life, Woolf's use of pet names, and the fantasies she built around this practice, was in part a means of achieving closeness with others. Hermione Lee, in an even-handed discussion of Woolf's relationship with her husband in her magnificent biography of the writer, notes how 'The pet names, the animal games, the "little beasts", the "marmots", coming out to play or being given an airing, the cuddling and nuzzling and kisses: these "antics" are often referred to in the letters and diaries of the early years.' Rather than being embarrassed by them, Lee sees this animal name-calling as 'evidence of a secret erotic life'.[42] Similarly, the correspondence which chronicles aspects of Woolf's relationship with Vita Sackville-West is as much about animals as humans. In this case, in addition to the identities of sheepdog and mole and squirrel mentioned earlier, real dogs and the interpretation of their behaviour act as surrogates for their owners, canine transgressions standing for human sexual and emotional activities. But Woolf also manages a less coy register which suggests an interest in exploring not just the cosiness of human intimacy, but bodies themselves. If one brings human and animal behaviour into proximity, Midgley maintains, one realizes, without anthropomorphizing the latter, that the behaviour of animals reveals 'expressive and interpretative capacities far older and far deeper than words', as, she claims, 'with human beings . . . we recognize [the] direct expression of emotion through conduct as more reliable than its expression through words, when the two conflict'.[43] This is apparent at the most direct sexual level, granting Woolf the licence to abandon reticence. 'To think of sporting with oysters', Woolf wrote to Vita after spending a night at Long Barn: '—lethargic glaucous lipped oysters, lewd lascivious oysters,—to think of it, I say . . . You only be a careful dolphin in your gambolling'—a choice of words that curiously but revealingly momentarily links Vita with Vanessa—'or you'll find Virginia's soft crevices lined with hooks'.[44]

Conflating humans and animals has its dangers, however. Woolf also knew that to hide behind pet names was to avoid talking one to one as adults, to avoid confronting human issues

[42] Hermione Lee, *Virginia Woolf* (London: Chatto & Windus, 1996), 332–3.
[43] Midgley, *Animals and Why They Matter*, 59.
[44] Virginia Woolf to Vita Sackville-West, 4 July 1927, in *Letters*, iii. 556.

as humans. It is noticeable, in fact, in *Flush*, that the spaniel's own independence to roam the streets, to make new dog friends and partnerships, comes after his bond with his mistress has been altered for ever by her marriage: the severance of the human–animal bond has been a necessary stage in emotional development on both sides. The dangers of living in the imaginary animal world come across particularly well in Woolf's late short story 'Lappin and Lapinova', published in *Harper's Bazaar* in 1939.[45] In it, the Thorburns, Rosalind and Ernest, share a private language, developed on honeymoon as they try to get used to the fact that they are, indeed, married to each other. Ernest is a 'King Rabbit'; Rosalind a hare. Their fantasy world sustains them; 'made them feel, more even than most young married couples, in league together against the rest of the world' (p. 354), giving them a silent and private connection when dinner-party conversations turn to hunting and shooting. But their marriage, never promising, grows stale; Ernest fails to respond to Rosalind's pathetic attempts to sustain conversation through an animal register. One evening, the sound of Ernest turning the key in the lock is like a shot:

'Sitting in the dark?' he said.

'Oh, Ernest, Ernest!' she cried, starting up in her chair.

'Well, what's up, now?' he asked briskly, warming his hands at the fire.

'It's Lapinova . . .' she faltered, glancing wildly at him out of her great startled eyes. 'She's gone, Ernest. I've lost her!'

Ernest frowned. He pressed his lips tight together. 'Oh, that's

---

[45] Virginia Woolf, 'Lappin and Lapinova', *Harper's Bazaar* (Apr. 1939), repr. in *The Complete Shorter Fiction*, ed. Susan Dick (London: Hogarth Press, 1985), 351–61. Subsequent page references in parentheses in the text.

what's up is it?' he said, smiling rather grimly at his wife. For ten seconds he stood there, silent; and she waited, feeling hands tightening at the back of her neck.

'Yes,' he said at length. 'Poor Lapinova . . .' He straightened his tie at the looking-glass over the mantelpiece.

'Caught in a trap,' he said, 'killed,' and sat down and read the newspaper.

So that was the end of that marriage (pp. 360–1).

Lee describes the story as delineating 'the death of a marriage when the erotic, escapist fantasy of the animal names is cruelly killed off by the husband',[46] but, rather, it may be read as Woolf expressing not just the vulnerability of fantasy life, but exposing its limitations; showing its evasions as well as the seductive self-protectionism of a private code. At the same time, she appropriates the connotations of the Thorburns' personal menagerie to make her more explicitly feminist point about the dangers, for a woman, of living in a world ruled by a consuming adherence to intimacy. Ernest's complicity in this amounts to him keeping his wife as a pet, yet one towards whom he refuses to adopt full responsibility and with whom —perhaps precisely because she is *not* an animal—he eventually gets bored.

When one moves into that third area in which Woolf engages with the animal world, the inter-species propensity towards cruelty and violence, her own arguments become passionately invested with feeling, with fear, at times even with prejudices at odds with the movements we have already observed towards a form of generous egalitarianism. This readiness to acknowledge and investigate violence and competition among animals becomes increasingly pronounced in

[46] Lee, *Virginia Woolf*, 333.

the 1930s. We encounter it in *The Waves*, where, in the italicized interludes which precede each of the temporal movements of the work, birds once again figure prominently. Initially they chirp, announcing sunrise; then they sing 'wildly', joyously, 'like skaters rollicking arm-in-arm'; their plumage showy, party-wear, 'specked canary and rose'.[47] But if these interludes progress according to a developmental model that parallels the life stages of the six protagonists, as they surely do, then it is notable that as Susan, Ginny, and Rhoda, Bernard, Neville, and Louis arrive at young adulthood, so the birds become far more sinister. They socialize, one might say, singing together 'as if conscious of companionship' (p. 58); swerving communally from the movement of the black cat—but they are also existing within a world where play and competition have become almost indistinguishable: 'escaping, pursuing, pecking each other as they turned high in the air' (pp. 58–9). They have now entered a world of violence, predatoriness, and selfish exploitation; worse still, they seem to derive an almost erotic, penetrative satisfaction from their habits of sustenance in a reversal of the fecundity and harmony of the garden of Eden:

Then one of them, beautifully darting, accurately alighting, spiked the soft, monstrous body of the defenceless worm, pecked again and yet again, and left it to fester. Down there among the roots where the flowers decayed, gusts of dead smells were wafted; drops formed on the bloated sides of swollen things. The skin of rotten fruit broke, and matter oozed too thick to run. Yellow excretions were exuded by slugs, and now and again an amorphous body with a head at either end swayed slowly from side to side. The gold-eyed birds darting in

---

[47] Virginia Woolf, *The Waves* (1931; Oxford: Oxford University Press, 1992), 21. Subsequent page references in parentheses in the text.

between the leaves observed that purulence, that wetness, quizzically. Now and then they plunged the tips of their beaks savagely into the sticky mixture (p. 59).

There is little distinction between them and the violence of the waves drumming on the shore, themselves like 'turbaned warriors, like turbaned men with poisoned assegais who, whirling their arms on high, advance upon the feeding flocks, the white sheep' (p. 60): violence here figured, despite the book's overt satire at the expense of colonialism through the figure of Percival, as a generic savage orientalism or africanism preying upon the innocent and peaceful, the safely grazing animal figures of Christian tradition.

Returning to the birds, Woolf hypothesizes the possibility of their aesthetic consciousness, a sharp bird's-eye view as they focus their golden eyes on one object in particular, as in *Flush*, a non-human, new angle of vision and perspective: 'Perhaps it was a snail shell, rising in the grass like a grey cathedral, a swelling building burnt with dark rings and shadowed green by the grass' (p. 59). Snail shells were a source of speculative fascination for Woolf, a starting-point for meditation in their self-contained intricate architecture, the miniature house that they represent: although 'the mark on the wall', in the prose piece of that name where she describes the 'flight of the mind' as it travels from association to association, is 'only a snail', something mundane and indeed—in an indoor environment—out of place, it has, simultaneously, been the focus for mental expansion taking its anonymous, unassuming exterior as a springboard. But if a snail shell suggests the potential for expansive life hidden within a hard exterior, so also it is vulnerable, smashable. Hence the birds in *The Waves* continue their hunting, just before the protagonists meet together in a London restaurant: 'They swooped suddenly from the lilac bough or the fence. They spied a snail and tapped the shell against a stone. They tapped furiously, methodically, until the shell broke and something slimy oozed from the crack' (p. 89). However, this is a reversible metaphor: rather than the cruel process of life performing violence on the individual, the individual may be the person inflicting the violence. Bernard takes up the same language: 'We who have been separated by our youth (the oldest is not yet twenty-five), who have sung like eager birds each his own song and tapped with the remorseless and savage egotism of the young our own snail-shell till it cracked (I am engaged)' (p. 101). This image simultaneously suggests that learning to break down the hard shell of our own identities, merging with others, is a part of what we ideally take on board in adult life, but it also hints at the condition of marriage: that one person's assertion may involve violating the space of another.

The aggression of animals, their competitiveness, their struggle for survival; the moment in which play spills over into something more serious and deadly: this is increasingly linked, by Woolf, with the energies that lead to war. In *Jacob's Room*, packed with proleptic references to the First World War which will kill Jacob, an old woman tells the young boy about the animals she sees from her cottage door: 'The fox cubs played in the gorse in the early morning, she told him. And if you looked out at dawn you could always see two badgers. Sometimes they knocked each other over like two boys fighting, she said' (p. 28); the point remaining un-spoken is that war is not play, and should not be entered into as though it's only a rehearsal of a fight to the death, like cubbish role-learning. Nature—encompassing the animal world—is neither a force offering a superior set of moral values to human ones, nor is it a repository of bestial violence that humans need to guard against slipping back into. Rather, it is envisaged by Woolf as the same for animals and humans. In the 'Time Passes' section of *To the Lighthouse*, making specific reference to the First World War, the narrator asks 'Did Nature supplement what man advanced? Did she complete what he began? With equal complacence she saw his misery, condoned his meanness, and acquiesced in his torture' (p. 182).

But if the same, then its more sinister aspects become the more apparent with the onset of the Second World War. Previously, the most overt apprehension about the correspondence between humans and predatory animals is vested in the thoughts of Septimus, in *Mrs Dalloway*, where we have the option of seeing his viewpoint as exaggerated, in the uncertain hinterland between sanity and insanity, when he observes that 'the truth is . . . that human beings have neither kindness, nor faith, nor charity beyond what serves to increase the pleasure of the moment. They hunt in packs. Their packs scour the desert and vanish screaming into the wildernesses' (pp. 116–17). The savagery of nature—the word 'savagery' is deliberately chosen—emerges above all in her final novel, *Between the Acts*. Here conflict is presented as inevitable: between humans, between sexes, between animals, between nations. On the last page, we learn that the warring couple, Isa and Giles, 'must fight, as the dog fox fights with the vixen, in the heart of darkness, in the fields of night'.[48] But is this in fact an

---

[48] Virginia Woolf, *Between the Acts* (1941; Oxford: Oxford University Press, 1992), 197. Subsequent page references in parentheses in the text.

inevitability, or—according to the logic of the novel—a sliding back of humanity into barbarism, the world of the beast: an abandonment of civilization, in which humans are ranged on one side, violent animals on the other? The idea of reversion, of 'reeling back into the beast', to use Tennyson's terrified Victorian formulation in *The Idylls of the King*, runs through *Between the Acts*. Mrs Swithin reads in her Outline of History of the prehistoric time in which the land was populated by 'elephant-bodied, seal-necked, heaving, surging, slowly writhing, and, she supposed, barking monsters; the iguanodon, the mammoth, and the mastodon; from whom presumably, she thought . . . we descend' (p. 8). In a notebook she kept whilst working on *Between the Acts*, Woolf describes 'London in War': 'Nature prevails. I suppose badgers & foxes wd. come back if this went on, & owls & nightingales. This is the prelude to barbarism.'[49] This fear is not new to Woolf's fiction. In *Mrs Dalloway*, Clarissa, experiencing intense hatred of Miss Kilman, hates, too, the troubling feelings that awareness of this hatred stirs up within her: 'It rasped her . . . to have stirring about in her this brutal monster! to hear twigs cracking and feel hooves planted down in the depths of that leaf-encumbered forest, the soul' (p. 15). Her hatred is like a 'brute' stirring, 'a monster grubbing at the roots' (p. 15) of her bodily (and her actual) home. This monster is not quite animal, not quite human; a primitive creature, a Caliban, inarticulate, making the primitive and the animal words indistinguishable (and once again, this vocabulary links her to Septimus, with his vision of the

---

[49] Virginia Woolf, 'London in War', Monk's House Papers A 20:5, University of Sussex Library.

horror that is Dr Holmes: 'Human nature, in short, was on him—the repulsive brute, with the blood-red nostrils' (p. 120)). But in *Between the Acts*, Woolf is no longer just concerned with private fears about what may lurk under the world's surface. She is asking a question with larger political consequences.[50] Is there any way of escaping the conflict to the death, inherent within a predatory animal world; any way to stop differing nations from destroying themselves? In a notorious passage, Giles comes across a snake on a path, 'choked with a toad in its mouth. The snake was unable to swallow; the toad was unable to die. A spasm made the ribs contract; blood oozed. It was birth the wrong way round— a monstrous inversion' (p. 89). Giles then shows his simultaneous kinship to this world of violence, and his human wish to impose hierarchical domination, by raising his foot and stamping snake and toad to death.

Woolf's early obituary of the dog Shag raises some basic questions about human relations with animals. She opens by acknowledging that 'There is some impertinence as well as some foolhardiness in the way in which we buy animals for so much gold and silver and call them ours,' and goes on to state that 'There is something, too, profane in the familiarity, half

---

[50] None the less, in *Mrs Dalloway* we see a parallelism in the imagery which suggests that more is at stake than instantly appears. Mrs Dalloway's self is not the only surface to be ruffled in the course of the book. As the smart car passes through London with its anonymous important occupant, some in shops think of the dead (of the war), of the flag, of Empire—whilst 'In a public-house in a back street a Colonial insulted the House of Windsor, which led to words, broken beer glasses, and a general shindy . . . For the surface agitation of the passing car as it sunk grazed something very profound' (22). Given the tenor of this novel, with its scathing remarks about imperialism, the implication is that the disturbance from below is not necessarily to be condemned: it is a disturbance which would be crucial, dislocating, and very probably to be desired in relation to Mrs Dalloway's socially self-contained world.

contemptuous, with which we treat our animals. We deliberately transplant a little bit of simple wild life, and make it grow up beside ours, which is neither simple nor wild . . . How have we the impertinence to make these wild creatures forego their nature for ours, which at best they can but imitate?'[51] Yet despite this questioning, Woolf goes on to co-opt animals for her own ends. These ends change, however, over her writing career. In *Between the Acts*, the elderly Lucy Swithin is satirized through the viewpoint of the younger generation, in the form of William and Isa: 'She was off, they guessed, on a circular tour of the imagination—one-making. Sheep, cows, grass, trees, ourselves—all are one. If discordant, producing harmony—if not to us, to a gigantic ear attached to a gigantic head. And thus—she was smiling benignly—the agony of the particular sheep, cow, or human being is necessary; and so— she was beaming seraphically at the gilt vane in the distance—we reach the conclusion that *all* is harmony, could we hear it. And we shall' (p. 157). But this harmony is no longer an option for Woolf. The animal world, like the human world, is divided against itself, in antagonism, and—the sweep of historical and prehistorical references in the novel suggest—this is a recurrent condition. Yet if the references to prehistory and the struggles for domination and survival which took place then function to demolish evolutionary ideas which are dependent on a teleological version of history, so, too, do they undermine the hierarchical layering of civilized and savage, based on a developmental model, which we see informing Woolf's earlier writing, at least unconsciously. Through the metaphor of birds, nations are now joined

[51] Virginia Woolf, 'On a Faithful Friend', *Guardian* (18 Jan. 1904), repr. in *The Essays of Virginia Woolf*, i. *1904–1912*, ed. Andrew McNeillie, 12.

horizontally, not vertically: swallows migrate between Africa and England and back again.

Woolf's arrival at this point is in part, necessarily, a function of contemporary politics, when it was no longer possible to sustain impartiality in the face of an ideological struggle that necessitated supporting war against the tyrannies of Fascism and Nazism, of regimes dedicated to selective exterminations, and the breeding of a 'pure race', in their drive for domination. No longer does the human species look like one species: action is needed to safeguard or regain the rights not just of those powerless to defend themselves, but indeed of many others besides. Moving out from this, one can see that Woolf's position by the end of her life calls into question the inclusiveness of the terms 'humans' and 'animals', an implied dichotomy—however much the borders are transgressed and elided—in which, as Suzanne Kappeler has put it in her article on 'Speciesism, Racism, Nationalism . . .',

the term 'animals' is used in a universalizing way, as if all animals were the same. Yet we know this to be a feature of all dichotomous and hierarchical oppositions, affecting the subordinate category: under the perspective of sexism, all women are 'the same,' exemplars of the sex and interchangeable; under the perspective of racism all black people are 'the same' and exchangeable.[52]

Expressing antagonism rather than harmony between species; focusing on the feral rather than on the petted and domestic: at first glance, this may resemble the point made earlier in relation to Woolf's fascination with the animal world, that to

---

[52] Suzanne Kappeler, 'Speciesism, Racism, Nationalism . . . or the Power of Scientific Subjectivity', in Adams and Donovan (eds.), *Animals & Women*, 330.

employ a zoomorphic linguistic register can be to signal fear, to express extremes of emotion which cannot be contained by reference to the human. But Woolf's final position should be read in a more challenging light. It is one which looks forwards to much more recent developments not just in general discussions about species and rights, but in debates about race and feminism: debates in which the question of difference is not founded upon the presumed absolutes of woman and man, black and white, human and animal, as much as on shifting power relations, specific histories, and intricate diversities; debates in which the decentring and pluralism which can be found in Woolf's co-optation of the animal world are increasingly crucial.

Flush, in other words, is much more than a playful writer's holiday, or a set of private jokes and allusions, or a money-spinner. Its radical potential, and the reason that we must take it seriously, lies in the fact that whilst it is all these things, it also makes us think about the very question of how values are constructed in our world. The book defamiliarizes the Victorian period through seeing it through canine eyes, even if the picture that it gives readers at the end of the twentieth century may seem a more familiar one than it did to Woolf's contemporaries—for, as Woolf so ably shows us, the overlooked and underrated perspective of a dog may be uncannily close to the underrated perspective of the thinking Victorian woman. Feminist criticism—and Woolf's writing in general has been enormously influential in the development of such criticism —has enabled us to reassess the Victorian period and its assumptions, even establishing something of a new orthodoxy when it comes to the outlines of its interpretation. But the fact that *Flush* has largely been written off by critics, pushed to the margins of Woolf's own work, should serve as a reminder that we are still in the habit of establishing hierarchies of value. Establishing the importance of this apparently light text opens up a range of questions which are woven through the whole of Woolf's writing: how different, how similar, are people of different sexes, members of different races, or creatures from different parts of the animal world? *Flush* suggests that we may be very wrong to take for granted those grounds on which we assume difference.

NOTE ON THE TEXT

Flush first appeared, serialized in its entirety, in the *Atlantic Monthly* for 1933: July, pp. 1–12; August, pp. 163–74; September, pp. 326–37; October, pp. 439–53.

The first edition was published by Leonard and Virginia Woolf at the Hogarth Press, 5 October 1933. It had a cream dust-jacket, printed in brown with an illustration of a dog. 12,680 copies were printed at 7s. 6d. (the 'Large Paper Edition'). A second impression of 3,000 copies was brought out later in October. The third to the fifth printing was issued as the Uniform Edition: 16 November 1933 (11,762 copies); January 1947 (3,400 copies), 1952 (3,000 copies). The second English edition appeared 20 September 1956, when 15,000 copies were published by Cassells; the third English edition 14 January 1960, when 7,500 copies were published by Methuen in their Venture Library.

The first American edition was published 5 October 1933, by Harcourt Brace Janovitch. 7,500 copies were printed, at $2 each. A white dust-jacket was printed in chrome yellow and black with an illustration of a dog. The book went to twelve reimpressions totalling 23,782 copies between October 1933 and January 1956. The Book of the Month Club Inc., New York, distributed copies to their members as an alternative selection in October 1933.

The manuscript of *Flush* is in the Henry W. and Albert A. Berg Collection at the New York Public Library, together with Woolf's reading notes. A draft of the first chapter is in one notebook, together with drafts of a number of essays, including early versions of those which were to be published as 'The London Scene'; a draft of the remaining chapters is in a further notebook, again together with other material, and a third notebook contains a later holograph draft of the entire text. The early drafts contain slightly more factual material —about London and about Elizabeth Barrett Browning —than the final text, which is the most canine-centred of Woolf's versions.

The text used here is that of the first British edition. Superscript numbers refer to Woolf's own notes at the end of the text; editorial notes follow, and are signalled by an asterisk in the text.

SELECT BIBLIOGRAPHY

Bibliography

Kirkpatrick, B. J., *A Bibliography of Virginia Woolf* (2nd edn.; Oxford: Oxford University Press, 1980).

Rice, Thomas J., *Virginia Woolf: A Guide to Research* (New York: Garland, 1984).

Biography

Bell, Quentin, *Virginia Woolf: A Biography* (2 vols.; London: Hogarth Press, 1972).

Lee, Hermione, *Virginia Woolf* (London: Chatto & Windus, 1996).

Mepham, John, *Virginia Woolf: A Literary Life* (London: Macmillan, 1991).

Rose, Phyllis, *Woman of Letters: A Life of Virginia Woolf* (London: Routledge, 1978).

Editions

The Collected Essays of Virginia Woolf, ed. Leonard Woolf (4 vols.; London: Hogarth Press, 1966, 1967).

The Complete Shorter Fiction, ed. Susan Dick (London: Hogarth Press, 1985).

The Diary of Virginia Woolf, ed. Anne Olivier Bell, assisted by Andrew McNeillie (5 vols.; London: Hogarth Press, 1977–84).

The Essays of Virginia Woolf, ed. Andrew McNeillie (London: Hogarth Press, 1986–   ).

The Letters of Virginia Woolf, ed. Nigel Nicolson and Joanne Trautmann (6 vols.; London: Hogarth Press, 1975–84).

Woolf, Virginia, *Women and Writing*, ed. and introd. Michèle Barrett (London: The Women's Press, 1979).

General Criticism

Beer, Gillian, *Arguing with the Past* (London: Routledge, 1989).

Bowlby, Rachel, *Virginia Woolf: Feminist Destinations* (Oxford: Blackwell, 1988).

Briggs, Julia (ed.), *Virginia Woolf: Introductions to the Major Works* (London: Virago, 1994).

Carroll, Berenice A., '"To Crush Him in Our Own Country": The Political Thought of Virginia Woolf', *Feminist Studies*, 4 (1978), 91–131.

DiBattista, Maria, *Virginia Woolf's Major Novels: The Fables of Anon* (New Haven: Yale University Press, 1980).

Hussey, Mark (ed.), *Virginia Woolf and War: Fiction, Reality, and Myth* (Syracuse: Syracuse University Press, 1991).

Joplin, Patricia Klindienst, 'The Authority of Illusion: Feminism and Fascism in Virginia Woolf's *Between the Acts*', *South Central Review*, 6 (1989), 88–104.

Laurence, Patricia Ondek, *The Reading of Silence: Virginia Woolf in the English Tradition* (Stanford, Calif.: Stanford University Press, 1991).

Marcus, Jane (ed.), *New Feminist Essays on Virginia Woolf* (London: Macmillan, 1981).

—— (ed.), *Virginia Woolf: A Feminist Slant*, (Lincoln, Nebr.: University of Nebraska Press, 1983).

—— *Virginia Woolf and the Languages of Patriarchy* (Bloomington, Ind.: Indiana University Press, 1987).

—— 'Britannia Rules *The Waves*', in K. R. Lawrence (ed.), *Decolonizing Tradition* (Urbana, Ill.: University of Illinois Press, 1992), 136–62.

Phillips, Kathy J., *Virginia Woolf against Empire* (Knoxville, Tenn.: University of Tennessee Press, 1994).

Transue, Pamela J., *Virginia Woolf and the Politics of Style* (New York: State University of New York Press, 1986).

Zwerdling, Alex, *Virginia Woolf and the Real World* (Berkeley and Los Angeles: University of California Press, 1986).

On Flush

Caughie, Pamela L., '*Flush* and the Literary Canon: Oh where oh where has that little dog gone?', *Tulsa Studies in Women's*

Literature, 10 (1991), 47–66.

Squier, Susan, *Virginia Woolf and London: The Sexual Politics of the City* (Chapel Hill, NC: University of North Carolina Press, 1985), especially chapter 6.

On Elizabeth Barrett Browning

Leighton, Angela, *Elizabeth Barrett Browning* (Brighton: Harvester Press, 1986).

Mermin, Dorothy, *Elizabeth Barrett Browning: The Origins of a New Poetry* (Chicago: University of Chicago Press, 1989).

Taplin, Gardner B., *The Life of Elizabeth Barrett Browning* (London: John Murray, 1957).

On Animals and Species

Adams, Carol J., and Donovan, Josephine (eds.), *Animals & Women: Feminist Theoretical Explorations* (Durham, NC: Duke University Press, 1995).

Baker, Steve, *Picturing the Beast: Animals, Identity, and Representation* (Manchester: Manchester University Press, 1993).

Birke, Lynda, *Feminism, Animals and Science: The Naming of the Shrew* (Buckingham: Open University Press, 1994).

Haraway, Donna, *Primate Visions: Gender, Race, and Nature in the World of Modern Science* (New York: Routledge, Chapman and Hall, 1989).

Midgley, Mary, *Animals and Why They Matter* (Athens, Ga: University of Georgia Press, 1984).

—— *Beast and Man: The Roots of Human Nature* (London: Routledge, rev. edn. 1995).

Ritvo, Harriet, *The Animal Estate: The English and Other Creatures in the Victorian Age* (London: Penguin Books, 1990).

Sheehan, James J., and Sosna, Morton, *The Boundaries of Humanity: Humans, Animals, Machines* (Berkeley and Los Angeles: University of California Press, 1991).

Woolf, Leonard, 'Fear and Politics: A Debate at the Zoo', in *Savage Times: Leonard Woolf on Peace and War*, introd. Stephen J. Stearns (New York: Garland Press, 1973).

A CHRONOLOGY OF VIRGINIA WOOLF

Life	*Historical and Cultural Background*
1882 (25 Jan.) Adeline Virginia Stephen (VW) born at 22 Hyde Park Gate, London.	Deaths of Darwin, Trollope, D. G. Rossetti; Joyce born; Stravinsky born; Married Women's Property Act; Society for Psychical Research founded.
1895 (5 May) Death of mother, Julia Stephen; VW's first breakdown occurs soon afterwards.	Death of T. H. Huxley; X-rays discovered; invention of the cinematograph; wireless telegraphy invented; arrest, trials, and conviction of Oscar Wilde. Wilde, *The Importance of Being Earnest* and *An Ideal Husband* Wells, *The Time Machine*
1896 (Nov.) Travels in France with sister Vanessa.	Death of William Morris; *Daily Mail* started. Hardy, *Jude the Obscure* Housman, *A Shropshire Lad*
1897 (10 April) Marriage of half-sister Stella; (19 July) death of Stella; (Nov.) VW learning Greek and History at King's College, London.	Queen Victoria's Diamond Jubilee; Tate Gallery opens. Stoker, *Dracula* James, *What Maisie Knew*
1898	Deaths of Gladstone and Lewis Carroll; radium and plutonium discovered. Wells, *The War of the Worlds*
1899 (30 Oct.) VW's brother Thoby goes up to Trinity College, Cambridge, where he forms friendships with Lytton Strachey, Leonard Woolf, Clive Bell, and others of the future Bloomsbury Group (VW's younger brother Adrian follows him to Trinity in 1902).	Boer War begins. Births of Bowen and Coward. Symons, *The Symbolist Movement in Literature* James, *The Awkward Age* Freud, *The Interpretation of Dreams*
1900	Deaths of Nietzsche, Wilde, and Ruskin; *Daily Express* started; Planck announces quantum theory; Boxer Rising. Conrad, *Lord Jim*

1901		Death of Queen Victoria; accession of Edward VII; first wireless communication between Europe and USA; 'World's Classics' series begun. Kipling, *Kim*
1902	VW starts private lessons in Greek with Janet Case.	End of Boer War; British Academy founded; *Encyclopaedia Britannica* (10th edn.); *TLS* started. Bennett, *Anna of the Five Towns* James, *The Wings of the Dove*
1903		Deaths of Gissing and Spencer; *Daily Mirror* started; Wright brothers make their first aeroplane flight; Emmeline Pankhurst founds Women's Social and Political Union. Butler, *The Way of All Flesh* James, *The Ambassadors* Moore, *Principia Ethica*
1904	(22 Feb.) Death of father, Sir Leslie Stephen. In spring, VW travels to Italy with Vanessa and friend Violet Dickinson. (10 May) VW has second nervous breakdown and is ill for three months. Moves to 46, Gordon Square. (14 Dec.) VW's first publication appears.	Deaths of Christina Rossetti and Chekhov; Russo-Japanese War; *Entente Cordiale* between Britain and France. Chesterton, *The Napoleon of Notting Hill* Conrad, *Nostromo* James, *The Golden Bowl*
1905	(March, April) Travels in Portugal and Spain. Writes reviews and teaches once a week at Morley College, London.	Einstein, *Special Theory of Relativity*; Sartre born. Shaw, *Major Barbara* and *Man and Superman* Wells, *Kipps* Forster, *Where Angels Fear to Tread*
1906	(Sept. and Oct.) Travels in Greece. (20 Nov.) death of Thoby Stephen.	Death of Ibsen; Beckett born; Liberal Government elected; Campbell-Bannerman Prime Minister; launch of HMS *Dreadnought*.
1907	(7 Feb.) Marriage of Vanessa to Clive Bell. VW moves with Adrian to 29 Fitzroy Square. At work on her first novel, 'Melymbrosia' (working title for *The Voyage Out*).	Auden born; Anglo-Russian Entente. Synge, *The Playboy of the Western World* Conrad, *The Secret Agent* Forster, *The Longest Journey*

[li]

1908 (Sept.) Visits Italy with the Bells.

Asquith Prime Minister; Old Age Pensions Act; Elgar's First Symphony.
Bennett, *The Old Wives' Tale*
Forster, *A Room with a View*
Chesterton, *The Man Who Was Thursday*

1909 (17 Feb.) Lytton Strachey proposes marriage. (30 March) First meets Lady Ottoline Morrell. (April) Visits Florence. (Aug.) Visits Bayreuth and Dresden.

Death of Meredith; 'People's Budget'; English Channel flown by Blériot.
Wells, *Tono-Bungay*
Masterman, *The Condition of England*
Marinetti, *Futurist Manifesto*

1910 (Jan.) Works for women's suffrage. (June–Aug.) Spends time in a nursing home at Twickenham.

Deaths of Edward VII, Tolstoy, and Florence Nightingale; accession of George V; *Encyclopaedia Britannica* (11th edn.); Roger Fry's Post-Impressionist Exhibition.
Bennett, *Clayhanger*
Forster, *Howards End*
Yeats, *The Green Helmet*
Wells, *The History of Mr Polly*

1911 (April) Travels to Turkey, where Vanessa is ill. (Nov.) Moves to 38 Brunswick Square, sharing house with Adrian, John Maynard Keynes, Duncan Grant, and Leonard Woolf.

National Insurance Act; Suffragette riots.
Conrad, *Under Western Eyes*
Wells, *The New Machiavelli*
Lawrence, *The White Peacock*

1912 Rents Asheham House. (Feb.) Spends some days in Twickenham nursing home. (10 Aug.) Marriage to Leonard Woolf. Honeymoon in Provence, Spain, and Italy. (Oct.) Moves to 13 Clifford's Inn, London.

Second Post-Impressionist Exhibition; Suffragettes active; strikes by dockers, coal-miners, and transport workers; Irish Home Rule Bill rejected by Lords; sinking of SS *Titanic*; death of Scott in the Antarctic; *Daily Herald* started. English translations of Chekhov and Dostoevsky begin to appear.

1913 (March) MS of *The Voyage Out* delivered to publisher. Unwell most of summer. (9 Sept.) Suicide attempt. Remains under care of nurses and husband for rest of year.

New Statesman started; Suffragettes active.
Lawrence, *Sons and Lovers*

1914	(16 Feb.) Last nurse leaves. Moves to Richmond, Surrey.	Irish Home Rule Bill passed by Parliament; First World War begins (4 Aug.); Dylan Thomas born. Lewis, *Blast* Joyce, *Dubliners* Yeats, *Responsibilities* Hardy, *Satires of Circumstance* Bell, *Art*
1915	Purchase of Hogarth House, Richmond. (26 March) *The Voyage Out* published. (April, May) Bout of violent madness; under care of nurses until November.	Death of Rupert Brooke; Einstein, *General Theory of Relativity*; Second Battle of Ypres; Dardanelles Campaign; sinking of SS *Lusitania*; air attacks on London. Ford, *The Good Soldier* Lawrence, *The Rainbow* Brooke, *1914 and Other Poems* Richardson, *Pointed Roofs*
1916	(17 Oct.) Lectures to Richmond branch of the Women's Co-operative Guild. Regular work for *TLS*.	Death of James; Lloyd George Prime Minister; First Battle of the Somme; Battle of Verdun; Gallipoli Campaign; Easter Rising in Dublin. Joyce, *A Portrait of the Artist as a Young Man*
1917	(July) Hogarth Press commences publication with *The Mark on the Wall*. VW begins work on *Night and Day*.	Death of Edward Thomas. Third Battle of Ypres (Passchendaele); T. E. Lawrence's campaigns in Arabia; USA enters the War; Revolution in Russia (Feb., Oct.); Balfour Declaration. Eliot, *Prufrock and Other Observations*
1918	Writes reviews and *Night and Day*; also sets type for the Hogarth Press. (15 Nov.) First meets T. S. Eliot.	Death of Owen; Second Battle of the Somme; final German offensive collapses; Armistice with Germany (11 Nov.); Franchise Act grants vote to women over 30; influenza pandemic kills millions. Lewis, *Tarr* Hopkins, *Poems* Strachey, *Eminent Victorians*
1919	(1 July) Purchase of Monk's House, Rodmell, Sussex. (20 Oct.) *Night and Day* published.	Treaty of Versailles; Alcock and Brown fly the Atlantic; National Socialists founded in Germany. Sinclair, *Mary Olivier* Shaw, *Heartbreak House*
1920	Works on journalism and *Jacob's Room*.	League of Nations established. Pound, *Hugh Selwyn Mauberley* Lawrence, *Women in Love* Eliot, *The Sacred Wood* Fry, *Vision and Design*

1921	(7 or 8 April) *Monday or Tuesday* published. Ill for summer months. (4 Nov.) Finishes *Jacob's Room*.	Irish Free State founded. Huxley, *Crome Yellow*
1922	(Jan. to May) Ill. (14 Dec.) First meets Vita Sackville-West. (24 Oct.) *Jacob's Room* published.	Bonar Law Prime Minister; Mussolini forms Fascist Government in Italy; death of Proust; *Encyclopaedia Britannica* (12th edn.); *Criterion* founded; BBC founded; Irish Free State proclaimed. Eliot, *The Waste Land* Galsworthy, *The Forsyte Saga* Joyce, *Ulysses* Mansfield, *The Garden Party* Wittgenstein, *Tractatus Logico-Philosophicus*
1923	(March, April) Visits Spain. Works on 'The Hours', the first version of *Mrs Dalloway*.	Baldwin Prime Minister; BBC radio begins broadcasting (Nov.); death of K. Mansfield.
1924	Purchase of lease on 52 Tavistock Square, Bloomsbury. Gives lecture that becomes 'Mr Bennett and Mrs Brown'. (8 Oct.) Finishes *Mrs Dalloway*.	First (minority) Labour Government; Ramsay MacDonald Prime Minister; deaths of Lenin, Kafka, and Conrad. Ford, *Some Do Not* Forster, *A Passage to India* O'Casey, *Juno and the Paycock* Coward, *The Vortex*
1925	(23 April) *The Common Reader* published. (14 May) *Mrs Dalloway* published. Ill during summer.	Gerhardie, *The Polyglots* Ford, *No More Parades* Huxley, *Those Barren Leaves* Whitehead, *Science and the Modern World*
1926	(Jan) Unwell with German measles. Writes *To the Lighthouse*.	General Strike (3–12 May); *Encyclopaedia Britannica* (13th edn.); first television demonstration. Ford, *A Man Could Stand Up* Tawney, *Religion and the Rise of Capitalism*
1927	(March, April) Travels in France and Italy. (5 May) *To the Lighthouse* published. (5 Oct.) Begins *Orlando*.	Lindburgh flies solo across the Atlantic; first 'talkie' films.
1928	(11 Oct.) *Orlando* published. Delivers lectures at Cambridge on which she bases *A Room of One's Own*.	Death of Hardy; votes for women over 21. Yeats, *The Tower* Lawrence, *Lady Chatterley's Lover* Waugh, *Decline and Fall* Sherriff, *Journey's End* Ford, *Last Post* Huxley, *Point Counter Point* Bell, *Civilization*

1929	(Jan.) Travels to Berlin. (24 Oct.) *A Room of One's Own* published.	2nd Labour Government, MacDonald Prime Minister; collapse of New York Stock Exchange; start of world economic depression. Graves, *Goodbye to All That* Aldington, *Death of a Hero* Green, *Living*
1930	(20 Feb.) First meets Ethel Smyth; (29 May) Finishes first version of *The Waves*.	Mass unemployment; television starts in USA; deaths of Lawrence and Conan Doyle. Auden, *Poems* Eliot, *Ash Wednesday* Waugh, *Vile Bodies* Coward, *Private Lives* Lewis, *Apes of God*
1931	(April) Car tour through France. (8 Oct.) *The Waves* published. Writes *Flush*.	Formation of National Government; abandonment of Gold Standard; death of Bennett; Japan invades China.
1932	(21 Jan.) Death of Lytton Strachey. (13 Oct.) *The Common Reader*, 2nd series, published. Begins *The Years*, at this point called 'The Pargiters'.	Roosevelt becomes President of USA; hunger marches start in Britain; *Scrutiny* starts. Huxley, *Brave New World*
1933	(May) Car tour of France and Italy. (5 Oct.) *Flush* published.	Deaths of Galsworthy and George Moore; Hitler becomes Chancellor of Germany. Orwell, *Down and Out in Paris and London* Wells, *The Shape of Things to Come.*
1934	Works on *The Years*. (9 Sept.) Death of Roger Fry.	Waugh, *A Handful of Dust* Graves, *I, Claudius* Beckett, *More Pricks than Kicks* Toynbee, *A Study of History*
1935	Rewrites *The Years*. (May) Car tour of Holland, Germany, and Italy.	George V's Silver Jubilee; Baldwin Prime Minister of National Government; Germany re-arms; Italian invasion of Abyssinia (Ethiopia). Isherwood, *Mr Norris Changes Trains* T. S. Eliot, *Murder in the Cathedral*
1936	(May–Oct.) Ill. Finishes *The Years*. Begins *Three Guineas*.	Death of George V; accession of Edward VIII; abdication crisis; accession of George VI; Civil War breaks out in Spain; first of the Moscow show trials; Germany re-occupies the Rhineland; BBC television begins (2 Nov); deaths of Chesterton, Kipling, and Housman. Orwell, *Keep the Aspidistra Flying*

1937 (15 March) *The Years* published. Begins *Roger Fry: A Biography*. (18 July) Death in Spanish Civil War of Julian Bell, son of Vanessa.

Chamberlain Prime Minister; destruction of Guernica; death of Barrie. Orwell, *The Road to Wigan Pier*

1938 (2 June) *Three Guineas* published. Works on *Roger Fry*, and begins to envisage *Between the Acts*.

German *Anschluss* with Austria; Munich agreement; dismemberment of Czechoslovakia; first jet engine. Beckett, *Murphy* Bowen, *The Death of the Heart* Greene, *Brighton Rock*

1939 VW moves to 37 Mecklenburgh Square, but lives mostly at Monk's House. Works on *Between the Acts*. Meets Freud in London.

End of Civil War in Spain; Russo-German pact; Germany invades Poland (Sept.); Britain and France declare war on Germany (3 Sept.); deaths of Freud, Yeats, and Ford. Joyce, *Finnegans Wake* Isherwood, *Goodbye to Berlin*

1940 (25 July) *Roger Fry* published. (10 Sept.) Mecklenburgh Square house bombed. (18 Oct.) witnesses the ruins of 52 Tavistock Square, destroyed by bombs. (23 Nov.) Finishes *Between the Acts*.

Germany invades north-west Europe; fall of France; evacuation of British troops from Dunkirk; Battle of Britain; beginning of 'the Blitz'; National Government under Churchill.

1941 (26 Feb.) Revises *Between the Acts*. Becomes ill. (28 March) Drowns herself in River Ouse, near Monk's House. (July) *Between the Acts* published.

Germany invades USSR; Japanese destroy US Fleet at Pearl Harbor; USA enters war; death of Joyce.

FLUSH

CONTENTS

CHAPTER I

THREE MILE CROSS

IT is universally admitted that the family from which the subject of this memoir claims descent is one of the greatest antiquity.* Therefore it is not strange that the origin of the name itself is lost in obscurity. Many million years ago the country which is now called Spain seethed uneasily in the ferment of creation. Ages passed; vegetation appeared; where there is vegetation the law of Nature has decreed that there shall be rabbits; where there are rabbits, Providence has ordained there shall be dogs. There is nothing in this that calls for question or comment. But when we ask why the dog that caught the rabbit was called a Spaniel, then doubts and difficulties begin. Some historians say that when the Carthaginians landed in Spain the common soldiers shouted with one accord 'Span! Span!'—for rabbits darted from every scrub, from every bush. The land was alive with rabbits. And *Span* in the Carthaginian tongue signifies Rabbit. Thus the land was called Hispania, or Rabbit-land,* and the dogs, which were almost instantly perceived in full pursuit of the rabbits, were called Spaniels or rabbit dogs.

There many of us would be content to let the matter rest; but truth compels us to add that there is another school of thought which thinks differently. The word Hispania, these scholars say, has nothing whatever to do with the Carthaginian word *span*. Hispania derives from the Basque word *españa*, signifying an edge or boundary. If that is so, rabbits, bushes,

[5]

dogs, soldiers—the whole of that romantic and pleasant picture, must be dismissed from the mind; and we must simply suppose that the Spaniel is called a spaniel because Spain is called España. As for the third school of antiquaries which maintains that just as a lover calls his mistress monster or monkey, so the Spaniards called their favourite dogs crooked or cragged (the word *españa* can be made to take these meanings) because a spaniel is notoriously the opposite—that is too fanciful a conjecture to be seriously entertained.

Passing over these theories, and many more which need not detain us here, we reach Wales in the middle of the tenth century. The spaniel is already there, brought, some say, by the Spanish clan of Ebhor or Ivor many centuries previously; and certainly by the middle of the tenth century a dog of high repute and value. 'The Spaniel of the King is a pound in value,' Howel Dha* laid it down in his Book of Laws. And when we remember what the pound could buy in the year AD 948—how many wives, slaves, horses, oxen, turkeys and geese—it is plain that the spaniel was already a dog of value and reputation. He had his place already by the King's side. His family was held in honour before those of many famous monarchs. He was taking his ease in palaces when the Plantagenets and the Tudors and the Stuarts were following other people's ploughs through other people's mud. Long before the Howards, the Cavendishes or the Russells* had risen above the common ruck of Smiths, Joneses and Tomkins, the spaniel family was a family distinguished and apart. And as the centuries took their way, minor branches broke off from the parent stem. By degrees, as English history pursues its course, there came into existence at least seven famous Spaniel families—the Clumber, the Sussex, the

Norfolk, the Black Field, the Cocker, the Irish Water and the English Water,* all deriving from the original spaniel of prehistoric days but showing distinct characteristics, and therefore no doubt claiming privileges as distinct. That there was an aristocracy of dogs by the time Queen Elizabeth was on the throne Sir Philip Sidney bears witness: '. . . greyhounds, Spaniels and Hounds', he observes, 'where-of the first might seem the Lords, the second the Gentlemen, and the last the Yeomen of dogs',* he writes in the *Arcadia*.

But if we are thus led to assume that the Spaniels followed human example, and looked up to Greyhounds as their superiors and considered Hounds beneath them, we have to admit that their aristocracy was founded on better reasons than ours. Such at least must be the conclusion of anyone who studies the laws of the Spaniel Club.* By that august body it is plainly laid down what constitute the vices of a spaniel, and what constitute its virtues. Light eyes, for example, are undesirable; curled ears are still worse; to be born with a light nose or a topknot is nothing less than fatal. The merits of the spaniel are equally clearly defined. His head must be smooth, rising without a too-decided stoop from the muzzle; the skull must be comparatively rounded and well developed with plenty of room for brain power; the eyes must be full but not gozzled;* the general expression must be one of intelligence and gentleness. The spaniel that exhibits these points is encouraged and bred from; the spaniel who persists in perpetuating topknots and light noses is cut off from the privileges and emoluments of his kind. Thus the judges lay down the law and, laying down the law, impose penalties and privileges which ensure that the law shall be obeyed.

But, if we now turn to human society, what chaos and

confusion meet the eye! No Club has any such jurisdiction upon the breed of man. The Heralds' College* is the nearest approach we have to the Spaniel Club. It at least makes some attempt to preserve the purity of the human family. But when we ask what constitutes noble birth—should our eyes be light or dark, our ears curled or straight, are topknots fatal, our judges merely refer us to our coats of arms. You have none perhaps. Then you are nobody. But once make good your claim to sixteen quarterings, prove your right to a coronet, and then they say you are not only born, but nobly born into the bargain. Hence it is that not a muffineer in all Mayfair lacks its lion couchant or its mermaid rampant. Even our linendrapers mount the Royal Arms above their doors, as though that were proof that their sheets are safe to sleep in. Everywhere rank is claimed and its virtues are asserted. Yet when we come to survey the Royal Houses of Bourbon, Hapsburg and Hohenzollern,* decorated with how many coronets and quarterings, couchant and rampant with how many lions and leopards, and find them now in exile, deposed from authority, judged unworthy of respect, we can but shake our heads and admit that the Judges of the Spaniel Club judged better. Such is the lesson that is enforced directly we turn from these high matters to consider the early life of Flush in the family of the Mitfords.

About the end of the eighteenth century a family of the famous spaniel breed was living near Reading in the house of a certain Dr Midford or Mitford.* That gentleman, in conformity with the canons of the Heralds' College, chose to spell his name with a *t*, and thus claimed descent from the Northumberland family of the Mitfords of Bertram Castle. His wife was a Miss Russell,* and sprang, if remotely, still decidedly

from the ducal house of Bedford. But the mating of Dr
Mitford's ancestors had been carried on with such wanton
disregard for principles that no bench of judges could have
admitted his claim to be well bred or have allowed him to
perpetuate his kind. His eyes were light; his ears were curled;
his head exhibited the fatal topknot. In other words, he was
utterly selfish, recklessly extravagant, worldly, insincere and
addicted to gambling. He wasted his own fortune, his wife's
fortune, and his daughter's* earnings. He deserted them in
his prosperity and sponged upon them in his infirmity. Two
points he had in his favour indeed, great personal beauty—he
was like an Apollo* until gluttony and intemperance changed
Apollo into Bacchus*—and he was genuinely devoted to dogs.
But there can be no doubt that, had there been a Man Club
corresponding to the Spaniel Club in existence, no spelling of
Mitford with a *t* instead of with a *d*, no calling cousins with the
Mitfords of Bertram Castle, would have availed to protect
him from contumely and contempt, from all the penalties of
outlawry and ostracism, from being branded as a mongrel man
unfitted to carry on his kind. But he was a human being.
Nothing therefore prevented him from marrying a lady of
birth and breeding, from living for over eighty years, from
having in his possession several generations of greyhounds
and spaniels and from begetting a daughter.

All researches have failed to fix with any certainty the exact
year of Flush's birth,* let alone the month or the day; but it is
likely that he was born some time early in the year 1842.* It is
also probable that he was directly descended from Tray*
(*c.* 1816), whose points, preserved unfortunately only in the
untrustworthy medium of poetry, prove him to have been a
red cocker spaniel of merit. There is every reason to think that

Flush was the son of that 'real old cocking spaniel' for whom Dr Mitford refused twenty guineas 'on account of his excellence in the field'.* It is to poetry, alas,* that we have to trust for our most detailed description of Flush himself as a young dog. He was of that particular shade of dark brown which in sunshine flashes 'all over into gold'. His eyes were 'startled eyes of hazel bland'. His ears were 'tasselled'; his 'slender feet' were 'canopied in fringes' and his tail was broad. Making allowance for the exigencies of rhyme and the inaccuracies of poetic diction, there is nothing here but what would meet with the approval of the Spaniel Club. We cannot doubt that Flush was a pure-bred Cocker of the red variety marked by all the characteristic excellences of his kind.

The first months of his life were passed at Three Mile Cross, a working man's cottage near Reading. Since the Mitfords had fallen on evil days—Kerenhappock* was the only servant—the chair-covers were made by Miss Mitford herself and of the cheapest material; the most important article of furniture seems to have been a large table; the most important room a large greenhouse—it is unlikely that Flush was surrounded by any of those luxuries, rain-proof kennels, cement walks, a maid or boy attached to his person, that would now be accorded a dog of his rank. But he throve; he enjoyed with all the vivacity of his temperament most of the pleasures and some of the licences natural to his youth and sex. Miss Mitford, it is true, was much confined to the cottage. She had to read aloud to her father hour after hour; then to play cribbage;* then, when at last he slumbered, to write and write and write at the table in the greenhouse in the attempt to pay their bills and settle their debts. But at last the longed-for moment would come. She thrust her papers aside, clapped a hat on her head, took her umbrella and set off for a walk across the fields with her dogs. Spaniels are by nature sympathetic; Flush, as his story proves, had an even excessive appreciation of human emotions. The sight of his dear mistress snuffing the fresh air at last, letting it ruffle her white hair and redden the natural freshness of her face, while the lines on her huge brow smoothed themselves out, excited him to gambols whose wildness was half sympathy with her own delight. As she strode through the long grass, so he leapt hither and thither, parting its green curtain. The cool globes of dew or rain broke in showers of iridescent spray about his nose; the earth, here hard, here soft, here hot, here cold, stung, teased and tickled the soft pads of his feet. Then what a variety of smells interwoven in subtlest combination thrilled his nostrils; strong smells of earth, sweet smells of flowers; nameless smells of leaf and bramble; sour smells as they crossed the road; pungent smells as they entered bean-fields. But suddenly down the wind came tearing a smell sharper, stronger, more lacerating than any—a smell that ripped across his brain stirring a thousand instincts, releasing a million memories—the smell of hare, the smell of fox. Off he flashed like a fish drawn in a rush through water further and further. He forgot his mistress; he forgot all human kind. He heard dark men cry 'Span! Span!' He heard whips crack. He raced; he rushed. At last he stopped bewildered; the incantation faded; very slowly, wagging his tail sheepishly, he trotted back across the fields to where Miss Mitford stood shouting 'Flush! Flush! Flush!' and waving her umbrella. And once at least the call was even more imperious; the hunting horn roused deeper instincts, summoned wilder and stronger emotions that transcended memory and obliterated grass, trees, hare, rabbit, fox in one wild shout of ecstasy. Love blazed her torch in his eyes; he heard the hunting horn of Venus.* Before he was well out of his puppyhood, Flush was a father.

Such conduct in a man even, in the year 1842, would have called for some excuse from a biographer; in a woman no excuse could have availed; her name must have been blotted in ignominy from the page. But the moral code of dogs, whether better or worse, is certainly different from ours, and there was nothing in Flush's conduct in this respect that requires a veil now, or unfitted him for the society of the purest and the chastest in the land then. There is evidence, that is to say, that the elder brother of Dr Pusey* was anxious to buy him. Deducing from the known character of Dr Pusey the probable character of his brother, there must have been something serious, solid, promising well for future excellence whatever might be the levity of the present in Flush even as a puppy. But a much more significant testimony to the attractive nature of his gifts is that, even though Mr Pusey wished to buy him, Miss Mitford refused to sell him. As she was at her wits' end for money, scarcely knew indeed what tragedy to spin, what annual to edit, and was reduced to the repulsive expedient of asking her friends for help, it must have gone hard with her to refuse the sum offered by the elder brother of Dr Pusey. Twenty pounds had been offered for Flush's father. Miss Mitford might well have asked ten or fifteen for Flush. Ten or fifteen pounds was a princely sum, a magnificent sum to have at her disposal. With ten or fifteen pounds she might have re-covered her chairs, she might have re-stocked her green-house, she might have bought herself an entire wardrobe, and 'I have not bought a bonnet, a cloak, a gown, hardly a pair of gloves', she wrote in 1842, 'for four years'.*

But to sell Flush was unthinkable. He was of the rare order of objects that cannot be associated with money. Was he not of the still rare kind that, because they typify what is spiritual, what is beyond price, become a fitting token of the disinterestedness of friendship; may be offered in that spirit to a friend, if one is lucky enough to have one, who is more like a daughter than a friend; to a friend who lies secluded all through the summer months in a back bedroom in Wimpole Street, to a friend who is no other than England's foremost poetess, the brilliant, the doomed, the adored Elizabeth Barrett* herself? Such were the thoughts that came more and more frequently to Miss Mitford as she watched Flush rolling and scampering in the sunshine; as she sat by the couch of Miss Barrett in her dark, ivy-shaded London bedroom. Yes; Flush was worthy of Miss Barrett; Miss Barrett was worthy of Flush. The sacrifice was a great one; but the sacrifice must be made. Thus, one day, probably in the early summer of the year 1842, a remarkable couple might have been seen taking their way down Wimpole Street—a very short, stout, shabby, elderly lady, with a bright red face and bright white hair, who led by the chain a very spirited, very inquisitive, very well-bred golden cocker spaniel puppy. They walked almost the whole length of the street until at last they paused at No. 50. Not without trepidation, Miss Mitford rang the bell.

Even now perhaps nobody rings the bell of a house in Wimpole Street without trepidation. It is the most august of London streets, the most impersonal. Indeed, when the world seems tumbling to ruin, and civilization rocks on its foundations, one has only to go to Wimpole Street; to pace that avenue; to survey those houses; to consider their uniformity; to marvel at the window curtains and their consistency; to admire the brass knockers and their regularity; to observe butchers tendering joints and cooks receiving them; to reckon the incomes of the inhabitants and infer their consequent submission to the laws of God and man—one has only to go to Wimpole Street and drink deep of the peace breathed by authority in order to heave a sigh of thankfulness that, while Corinth has fallen and Messina has tumbled,* while crowns have blown down the wind and old Empires have gone up in flames, Wimpole Street has remained unmoved, and, turning from Wimpole Street into Oxford Street, a prayer rises in the heart and bursts from the lips that not a brick of Wimpole Street may be re-pointed, not a curtain washed, not a butcher fail to tender or a cook to receive the sirloin, the haunch, the breast, the ribs of mutton and beef for ever and ever, for as long as Wimpole Street remains, civilization is secure.

The butlers of Wimpole Street move ponderously even to-day; in the summer of 1842 they were more deliberate still. The laws of livery were then more stringent; the ritual of the green baize apron for cleaning silver; of the striped waistcoat and swallow-tail black coat for opening the hall door, was more closely observed. It is likely then that Miss Mitford and Flush were kept waiting at least three minutes and a half on the door-step. At last, however, the door of number fifty was flung wide; Miss Mitford and Flush were ushered in. Miss Mitford was a frequent visitor; there was nothing to surprise, though something to subdue her, in the sight of the Barrett family mansion. But the effect upon Flush must have been overwhelming in the extreme. Until this moment he had set foot in no house but the working man's cottage at Three Mile Cross. The boards there were bare; the mats were frayed; the chairs were cheap. Here there was nothing bare, nothing frayed, nothing cheap—that Flush could see at a glance. Mr Barrett, the owner, was a rich merchant; he had a large family of grown-up sons and daughters, and a retinue, proportionately large, of servants. His house was furnished in the fashion of the late 'thirties, with some tincture, no doubt, of that Eastern fantasy which had led him when he built a house in Shropshire* to adorn it with the domes and crescents of Moorish architecture. Here in Wimpole Street such extravagance would not be allowed; but we may suppose that the high dark rooms were full of ottomans and carved mahogany; tables were twisted; filigree ornaments stood upon them; daggers and swords hung upon wine-dark walls; curious objects brought from his East Indian property* stood in recesses, and thick rich carpets clothed the floors.

But as Flush trotted up behind Miss Mitford, who was behind the butler, he was more astonished by what he smelt than by what he saw. Up the funnel of the staircase came warm whiffs of joints roasting, of fowls basting, of soups simmering—ravishing almost as food itself to nostrils used to the meagre savour of Kerenhappock's penurious fries and hashes. Mixing with the smell of food were further smells —smells of cedarwood and sandalwood and mahogany; scents of male bodies and female bodies; of men servants and maid servants; of coats and trousers; of crinolines and mantles; of curtains of tapestry, of curtains of plush; of coal dust and fog; of wine and cigars. Each room as he passed it—dining-room, drawing-room, library, bedroom—wafted out its own contribution to the general stew; while, as he set down first one paw and then another, each was caressed and retained by the sensuality of rich pile carpets closing amorously over it. At length they reached a closed door at the back of the house. A gentle tap was given; gently the door was opened.

Miss Barrett's bedroom—for such it was—must by all accounts have been dark. The light, normally obscured by a curtain of green damask, was in summer further dimmed by the ivy, the scarlet runners, the convolvuluses and the nasturtiums which grew in the window-box. At first Flush could distinguish nothing in the pale greenish gloom but five white globes glimmering mysteriously in mid-air. But again it was the smell of the room that overpowered him. Only a scholar who has descended step by step into a mausoleum and there finds himself in a crypt, crusted with fungus, slimy with mould, exuding sour smells of decay and antiquity, while half-obliterated marble busts gleam in mid-air and all is dimly seen by the light of the small swinging lamp which he holds, and dips and turns, glancing now here, now there—only the sensations of such an explorer into the buried vaults of a ruined city can compare with the riot of emotions that flooded Flush's nerves as he stood for the first time in an invalid's bedroom, in Wimpole Street, and smelt eau-de-Cologne.

Very slowly, very dimly, with much sniffing and pawing, Flush by degrees distinguished the outlines of several articles of furniture. That huge object by the window was perhaps a wardrobe. Next to it stood, conceivably, a chest of drawers. In the middle of the room swam up to the surface what seemed to be a table with a ring round it; and then the vague amorphous shapes of armchair and table emerged. But everything was disguised. On top of the wardrobe stood three white busts; the chest of drawers was surmounted by a bookcase; the bookcase was pasted over with crimson merino; the washing-table had a coronal of shelves upon it; on top of the shelves that were on top of the washing-table stood two more busts. Nothing in the room was itself; everything was something else. Even the window-blind was not a simple muslin blind; it was a painted fabric[1] with a design of castles and gateways and groves of trees, and there were several peasants taking a walk. Looking-glasses further distorted these already distorted objects so that there seemed to be ten busts of ten poets instead of five; four tables instead of two. And suddenly there was a more terrifying confusion still. Suddenly Flush saw staring back at him from a hole in the wall another dog with bright eyes flashing, and tongue lolling! He paused amazed. He advanced in awe.

Thus advancing, thus withdrawing, Flush scarcely heard, save as the distant drone of wind among the tree-tops, the murmur and patter of voices talking. He pursued his investigations, cautiously, nervously, as an explorer in a forest softly advances his foot, uncertain whether that shadow is a lion, or that root a cobra. At last, however, he was aware of huge objects in commotion over him; and, unstrung as he was by the experiences of the past hour, he hid himself, trembling, behind a screen. The voices ceased. A door shut. For one instant he paused, bewildered, unstrung. Then with a pounce as of clawed tigers memory fell upon him. He felt himself alone—deserted. He rushed to the door. It was shut. He pawed, he listened. He heard footsteps descending. He knew them for the familiar footsteps of his mistress. They stopped. But no—on they went, down they went. Miss Mitford was slowly, was heavily, was reluctantly descending the stairs. And as she went, as he heard her footsteps fade, panic seized upon him. Door after door shut in his face as Miss Mitford went downstairs; they shut on freedom; on fields; on hares; on grass; on his adored, his venerated mistress—on the dear old woman who had washed him and beaten him and fed him from her own plate when she had none too much to eat herself—on all he had known of happiness and love and human goodness! There! The front door slammed. He was alone. She had deserted him.

Then such a wave of despair and anguish overwhelmed him, the irrevocableness and implacability of fate so smote him, that he lifted up his head and howled aloud. A voice said 'Flush'. He did not hear it. 'Flush', it repeated a second time. He started. He had thought himself alone. He turned. Was there something alive in the room with him? Was there something on the sofa? In the wild hope that this being, whatever it was, might open the door, that he might still rush after Miss Mitford and find her—that this was some game of hide-and-seek such as they used to play in the greenhouse at home—Flush darted to the sofa.

'Oh, Flush!' said Miss Barrett. For the first time she looked him in the face. For the first time Flush looked at the lady lying on the sofa.

Each was surprised. Heavy curls hung down on either side of Miss Barrett's face; large bright eyes shone out; a large mouth smiled. Heavy ears hung down on either side of Flush's face; his eyes, too, were large and bright: his mouth was wide. There was a likeness between them. As they gazed at each other each felt: Here am I—and then each felt: But how different! Hers was the pale worn face of an invalid, cut off from air, light, freedom. His was the warm ruddy face of a young animal; instinct with health and energy. Broken asunder, yet made in the same mould, could it be that each completed what was dormant in the other? She might have been—all that; and he—But no. Between them lay the widest

gulf that can separate one being from another. She spoke. He
was dumb. She was woman; he was dog. Thus closely united,
thus immensely divided, they gazed at each other. Then with
one bound Flush sprang on to the sofa and laid himself where
he was to lie for ever after—on the rug at Miss Barrett's feet.

CHAPTER II

THE BACK BEDROOM

THE summer of 1842 was, as historians tell us, not much different from other summers, yet to Flush it was so different that he must have doubted if the world itself were the same. It was a summer spent in a bedroom; a summer spent with Miss Barrett. It was a summer spent in London, spent in the heart of civilization. At first he saw nothing but the bedroom and its furniture, but that alone was surprising enough. To identify, distinguish and call by their right names all the different articles he saw there was confusing enough. And he had scarcely accustomed himself to the tables, to the busts, to the washing-stands—the smell of eau-de-Cologne still affected his nostrils disagreeably, when there came one of those rare days which are fine but not windy, warm but not baking, dry but not dusty, when an invalid can take the air. The day came when Miss Barrett could safely risk the huge adventure of going shopping with her sister.

The carriage was ordered; Miss Barrett rose from her sofa; veiled and muffled, she descended the stairs. Flush of course went with her. He leapt into the carriage by her side. Couched on her lap, the whole pomp of London at its most splendid burst on his astonished eyes. They drove along Oxford Street. He saw houses made almost entirely of glass.* He saw windows laced across with glittering streamers; heaped with gleaming mounds of pink, purple, yellow, rose. The carriage stopped. He entered mysterious arcades filmed with clouds and webs of tinted gauze. A million airs from China, from Arabia, wafted their frail incense into the remotest fibres of his senses. Swiftly over the counters flashed yards of gleaming silk; more darkly, more slowly rolled the ponderous bomba-zine. Scissors snipped; coins sparkled. Paper was folded; string tied. What with nodding plumes, waving streamers, tossing horses, yellow liveries, passing faces, leaping, dancing up, down, Flush, satiated with the multiplicity of his sensations, slept, drowsed, dreamt and knew no more until he was lifted out of the carriage and the door of Wimpole Street shut on him again.

And next day, as the fine weather continued, Miss Barrett ventured upon an even more daring exploit—she had herself drawn up Wimpole Street in a bath-chair. Again Flush went with her. For the first time he heard his nails click upon the hard paving-stones of London. For the first time the whole battery of a London street on a hot summer's day assaulted his nostrils. He smelt the swooning smells that lie in the gutters; the bitter smells that corrode iron railings; the fuming, heady smells that rise from basements—smells more complex, corrupt, violently contrasted and compounded than any he had smelt in the fields near Reading; smells that lay far beyond the range of the human nose; so that while the chair went on, he stopped, amazed; defining, savouring, until a jerk at his collar dragged him on. And also, as he trotted up Wimpole Street behind Miss Barrett's chair he was dazed by the passage of human bodies. Petticoats swished at his head; trousers brushed his flanks; sometimes a wheel whizzed an inch from his nose; the wind of destruction roared in his ears and fanned the feathers of his paws as a van passed. Then he plunged in terror. Mercifully the chain tugged at his collar:

Miss Barrett held him tight, or he would have rushed to destruction.

At last, with every nerve throbbing and every sense singing, he reached Regent's Park. And then when he saw once more, after years of absence it seemed, grass, flowers and trees, the old hunting cry of the fields hallooed in his ears and he dashed forward to run as he had run in the fields at home. But now a heavy weight jerked at his throat; he was thrown back on his haunches. Were there not trees and grass? he asked. Were these not the signals of freedom? Had he not always leapt forward directly Miss Mitford started on her walk? Why was he a prisoner here? He paused. Here, he observed, the flowers were massed far more thickly than at home; they stood, plant by plant, rigidly in narrow plots. The plots were intersected by hard black paths. Men in shiny top-hats marched ominously up and down the paths. At the sight of them he shuddered closer to the chair. He gladly accepted the protection of the chain. Thus before many of these walks were over a new conception had entered his brain. Setting one thing beside another, he had arrived at a conclusion. Where there are flower-beds there are asphalt paths; where there are flower-beds and asphalt paths and men in shiny top-hats, dogs must be led on chains. Without being able to decipher a word of the placard at the Gate, he had learnt his lesson—in Regent's Park dogs must be led on chains.

And to this nucleus of knowledge, born from the strange experiences of the summer of 1842, soon adhered another; dogs are not equal, but different. At Three Mile Cross Flush had mixed impartially with tap-room dogs and the Squire's greyhounds; he had known no difference between the tinker's dog and himself. Indeed it is probable that the mother of his child, though by courtesy called Spaniel, was nothing but a mongrel, eared in one way, tailed in another. But the dogs of London, Flush soon discovered, are strictly divided into different classes. Some are chained dogs; some run wild. Some take their airings in carriages and drink from purple jars; others are unkempt and uncollared and pick up a living in the gutter. Dogs therefore, Flush began to suspect, differ; some are high, others low; and his suspicions were confirmed by snatches of talk held in passing with the dogs of Wimpole Street. 'See that scallywag? A mere mongrel! . . . By gad, that's a fine Spaniel. One of the best blood in Britain! . . . Pity his ears aren't a shade more curly . . . There's a topknot for you!'

From such phrases, from the accent of praise or derision in which they were spoken, at the pillar-box or outside the public-house where the footmen were exchanging racing tips, Flush knew before the summer had passed that there is no equality among dogs: some dogs are high dogs; some are low. Which, then, was he? No sooner had Flush got home than he examined himself carefully in the looking-glass. Heaven be praised, he was a dog of birth and breeding! His head was smooth; his eyes were prominent but not gozzled; his feet were feathered; he was the equal of the best-bred cocker in Wimpole Street. He noted with approval the purple jar from which he drank—such are the privileges of rank; he bent his head quietly to have the chain fixed to his collar—such are its penalties. When about this time Miss Barrett observed him staring in the glass, she was mistaken. He was a philosopher, she thought, meditating the difference between appearance and reality. On the contrary, he was an aristocrat considering his points.

But the fine summer days were soon over; the autumn winds began to blow; and Miss Barrett settled down to a life of complete seclusion in her bedroom. Flush's life was also changed. His outdoor education was supplemented by that of the bedroom, and this, to a dog of Flush's temperament, was the most drastic that could have been invented. His only airings, and these were brief and perfunctory, were taken in the company of Wilson, Miss Barrett's maid.* For the rest of the day he kept his station on the sofa at Miss Barrett's feet. All his natural instincts were thwarted and contradicted. When the autumn winds had blown last year in Berkshire he had run in wild scampering across the stubble; now at the sound of the ivy tapping on the pane Miss Barrett asked Wilson to see to the fastenings of the window. When the leaves of the scarlet runners and nasturtiums in the window-box yellowed and fell she drew her Indian shawl more closely round her. When the October rain lashed the window Wilson lit the fire and heaped up the coals. Autumn deepened into winter and the first fogs jaundiced the air. Wilson and Flush could scarcely grope their way to the pillar-box or to the chemist. When they came back, nothing could be seen in the room but the pale busts glimmering wanly on the tops of the wardrobes; the peasants and the castle had vanished on the blind; blank yellow filled the pane. Flush felt that he and Miss Barrett lived alone together in a cushioned and firelit cave. The traffic droned on perpetually outside with muffled reverberations; now and again a voice went calling hoarsely, 'Old chairs and baskets to mend', down the street: sometimes there was a jangle of organ music, coming nearer and louder; going further and fading away. But none of these sounds meant freedom, or action, or exercise. The wind and the rain, the wild days of autumn and the cold days of mid-winter, all alike meant nothing to Flush except warmth and stillness; the lighting of lamps, the drawing of curtains and the poking of the fire.

At first the strain was too great to be borne. He could not help dancing round the room on a windy autumn day when the partridges must be scattering over the stubble. He thought he heard guns on the breeze. He could not help running to the door with his hackles raised when a dog barked outside. And yet when Miss Barrett called him back, when she laid her hand on his collar, he could not deny that another feeling, urgent, contradictory, disagreeable—he did not know what to call it or why he obeyed it—restrained him. He lay still at her feet. To resign, to control, to suppress the most violent instincts of his nature—that was the prime lesson of the bedroom school, and it was one of such portentous difficulty that many scholars have learnt Greek with less—many battles have been won that cost their generals not half such pain. But then, Miss Barrett was the teacher. Between them, Flush felt more and more strongly, as the weeks wore on, was a bond, an uncomfortable yet thrilling tightness; so that if his pleasure was her pain, then his pleasure was pleasure no longer but three parts pain. The truth of this was proved every day. Somebody opened the door and whistled him to come. Why should he not go out? He longed for air and exercise; his limbs were cramped with lying on the sofa. He had never grown altogether used to the smell of eau-de-Cologne. But no —though the door stood open, he would not leave Miss Barrett. He hesitated half-way to the door and then went back to the sofa. 'Flushie,' wrote Miss Barrett, 'is my friend—my companion—and loves me better than he loves the sunshine without.'* She could not go out. She was chained to the sofa. 'A bird in a cage would have as good a story',* she wrote, as she had. And Flush, to whom the whole world was free, chose to forfeit all the smells of Wimpole Street in order to lie by her side.

And yet sometimes the tie would almost break; there were vast gaps in their understanding. Sometimes they would lie and stare at each other in blank bewilderment. Why, Miss Barrett wondered, did Flush tremble suddenly, and whimper and start and listen? She could hear nothing; she could see nothing; there was nobody in the room with them. She could not guess that Folly, her sister's little King Charles, had passed the door; or that Catiline the Cuba bloodhound had been given a mutton-bone by a footman in the basement. But Flush knew; he heard; he was ravaged by the alternate rages of lust and greed. Then with all her poet's imagination Miss Barrett could not divine what Wilson's wet umbrella meant to Flush; what memories it recalled, of forests and parrots and wild trumpeting elephants; nor did she know, when Mr Kenyon* stumbled over the bell-pull, that Flush heard dark men cursing in the mountains; the cry, 'Span! Span!' rang in his ears, and it was in some muffled, ancestral rage that he bit him.

Flush was equally at a loss to account for Miss Barrett's emotions. There she would lie hour after hour passing her hand over a white page with a black stick; and her eyes would suddenly fill with tears; but why? 'Ah, my dear Mr Horne', she was writing. 'And then came the failure in my health . . . and then the enforced exile to Torquay . . . which gave a nightmare to my life for ever, and robbed it of more than I can speak of here; do not speak of that anywhere. *Do not speak of* *that*, dear Mr Horne.'* But there was no sound in the room, no smell to make Miss Barrett cry. Then again Miss Barrett, still agitating her stick, burst out laughing. She had drawn 'a very neat and characteristic portrait of Flush, humorously made rather like myself', and she had written under it that it 'only fails of being an excellent substitute for mine through being more worthy than I can be counted'.* What was there to laugh at in the black smudge that she held out for Flush to look at? He could smell nothing; he could hear nothing. There was nobody in the room with them. The fact was that they could not communicate with words, and it was a fact that led undoubtedly to much misunderstanding. Yet did it not lead also to a peculiar intimacy? 'Writing', Miss Barrett once exclaimed after a morning's toil, 'writing, writing . . .'* After all, she may have thought, do words say everything? Can words say anything? Do not words destroy the symbol that lies beyond the reach of words? Once at least Miss Barrett seems to have found it so. She was lying, thinking; she had forgotten Flush altogether, and her thoughts were so sad that the tears fell upon the pillow. Then suddenly a hairy head was pressed against her; large bright eyes shone in hers; and she started. Was it Flush, or was it Pan?* Was she no longer an invalid in Wimpole Street, but a Greek nymph in some dim grove in Arcady? And did the bearded god himself press his lips to hers? For a moment she was transformed; she was a nymph and Flush was Pan. The sun burnt and love blazed. But suppose Flush had been able to speak—would he not have said something sensible about the potato disease in Ireland?*

So, too, Flush felt strange stirrings at work within him. When he saw Miss Barrett's thin hands delicately lifting some silver box or pearl ornament from the ringed table, his own

furry paws seemed to contract and he longed that they should
fine themselves to ten separate fingers. When he heard her low
voice syllabling innumerable sounds, he longed for the day
when his own rough roar would issue like hers in the little
simple sounds that had such mysterious meaning. And when
he watched the same fingers for ever crossing a white page
with a straight stick, he longed for the time when he too
should blacken paper as she did.

And yet, had he been able to write as she did?—The
question is superfluous happily, for truth compels us to say
that in the year 1842–43 Miss Barrett was not a nymph but an
invalid; Flush was not a poet but a red cocker spaniel; and
Wimpole Street was not Arcady but Wimpole Street.

So the long hours went by in the back bedroom with
nothing to mark them but the sound of steps passing on the
stairs; and the distant sound of the front door shutting, and
the sound of a broom tapping, and the sound of the postman
knocking. In the room coals clicked; the lights and shadows
shifted themselves over the brows of the five pale busts, over
the bookcase and its red merino. But sometimes the step on
the stair did not pass the door; it stopped outside. The handle
was seen to spin round; the door actually opened; somebody
came in. Then how strangely the furniture changed its look!
What extraordinary eddies of sound and smell were at once set
in circulation! How they washed round the legs of tables and
impinged on the sharp edges of the wardrobe! Probably it was
Wilson, with a tray of food or a glass of medicine; or it might
be one of Miss Barrett's two sisters—Arabel or Henrietta; or
it might be one of Miss Barrett's seven brothers—Charles,
Samuel, George, Henry, Alfred, Septimus or Octavius. But
once or twice a week Flush was aware that something more

important was about to happen. The bed would be carefully disguised as a sofa. The armchair would be drawn up beside it; Miss Barrett herself would be wrapped becomingly in Indian shawls; the toilet things would be scrupulously hidden under the busts of Chaucer and Homer; Flush himself would be combed and brushed. At about two or three in the afternoon there was a peculiar, distinct and different tap at the door. Miss Barrett flushed, smiled and stretched out her hand. Then in would come—perhaps dear Miss Mitford, rosy and shiny and chattering, with a bunch of geraniums. Or it might be Mr Kenyon, a stout, well-groomed elderly gentleman, radiating benevolence, provided with a book. Or it might be Mrs Jameson,* a lady who was the very opposite of Mr Kenyon to look at—a lady with 'a very light complexion —pale, lucid eyes; thin colourless lips . . . a nose and chin projective without breadth'.* Each had his or her own manner, smell, tone and accent. Miss Mitford burbled and chattered, was fly-away yet substantial; Mr Kenyon was urbane and cultured and mumbled slightly because he had lost two front teeth;² Mrs Jameson had lost none of her teeth, and moved as sharply and precisely as she spoke.

Lying couched at Miss Barrett's feet, Flush let the voices ripple over him, hour by hour. On and on they went. Miss Barrett laughed, expostulated, exclaimed, sighed too, and laughed again. At last, greatly to Flush's relief, little silences came—even in the flow of Miss Mitford's conversation. Could it be seven already? She had been there since midday! She must really run to catch her train. Mr Kenyon shut his book—he had been reading aloud—and stood with his back to the fire; Mrs Jameson with a sharp, angular movement pressed each finger of her glove sharp down. And Flush was patted by this one and had his ear pulled by another. The routine of leave-taking was intolerably prolonged; but at last Mrs Jameson, Mr Kenyon, and even Miss Mitford had risen, had said good-bye, had remembered something, had lost something, had found something, had reached the door, had opened it, and were—Heaven be praised—gone at last.

Miss Barrett sank back very white, very tired on her pillows. Flush crept closer to her. Mercifully they were alone again. But the visitor had stayed so long that it was almost dinner-time. Smells began to rise from the basement. Wilson was at the door with Miss Barrett's dinner on a tray. It was set down on the table beside her and the covers lifted. But what with the dressing and the talking, what with the heat of the room and the agitation of the farewells, Miss Barrett was too tired to eat. She gave a little sigh when she saw the plump mutton chop, or the wing of partridge or chicken that had been sent up for her dinner. So long as Wilson was in the room she fiddled about with her knife and fork. But directly the door was shut and they were alone, she made a sign. She held up her fork. A whole chicken's wing was impaled upon it. Flush advanced. Miss Barrett nodded. Very gently, very cleverly, without spilling a crumb, Flush removed the wing; swallowed it down and left no trace behind. Half a rice pudding clotted with thick cream went the same way. Nothing could have been neater, more effective than Flush's co-operation.* He was lying couched as usual at Miss Barrett's feet, apparently asleep, Miss Barrett was lying rested and restored, apparently having made an excellent dinner, when once more a step that was heavier, more deliberate and firmer than any other, stopped on the stair; solemnly a knock sounded that was no tap of enquiry but a demand for admittance; the door opened and in came the blackest, the most formidable of elderly men—Mr Barrett himself. His eye at once sought the tray. Had the meal been eaten? Had his commands been obeyed? Yes, the plates were empty. Signifying his approval of his daughter's obedience, Mr Barrett lowered himself heavily into the chair by her side. As that dark body approached him, shivers of terror and horror ran down Flush's spine. So a savage couched in flowers shudders when the thunder growls and he hears the voice of God. Then Wilson whistled; and Flush, slinking guiltily, as if Mr Barrett could read his thoughts and those thoughts were evil, crept out of the room and rushed downstairs. A force had entered the bedroom which he dreaded; a force that he was powerless to withstand. Once he burst in unexpectedly. Mr Barrett was on his knees praying by his daughter's side.

CHAPTER III

THE HOODED MAN

SUCH an education as this, in the back bedroom at Wimpole Street, would have told upon an ordinary dog. And Flush was not an ordinary dog. He was high-spirited, yet reflective; canine, but highly sensitive to human emotions also. Upon such a dog the atmosphere of the bedroom told with peculiar force. We cannot blame him if his sensibility was cultivated rather to the detriment of his sterner qualities. Naturally, lying with his head pillowed on a Greek lexicon, he came to dislike barking and biting; he came to prefer the silence of the cat to the robustness of the dog; and human sympathy to either. Miss Barrett, too, did her best to refine and educate his powers still further. Once she took a harp from the window and asked him, as she laid it by his side, whether he thought that the harp, which made music, was itself alive? He looked and listened; pondered, it seemed, for a moment in doubt and then decided that it was not. Then she would make him stand with her in front of the looking-glass and ask him why he barked and trembled. Was not the little brown dog opposite himself? But what is 'oneself'? Is it the thing people see? Or is it the thing one is? So Flush pondered that question too, and, unable to solve the problem of reality, pressed closer to Miss Barrett and kissed her 'expressively'.* *That* was real at any rate.

Fresh from such problems, with such emotional dilemmas agitating his nervous system, he went downstairs, and we cannot be surprised if there was something—a touch of the supercilious, of the superior—in his bearing that roused the rage of Catiline, the savage Cuba bloodhound, so that he set upon him and bit him and sent him howling upstairs to Miss Barrett for sympathy. Flush 'is no hero',* she concluded; but why was he no hero? Was it not partly on her account? She was too just not to realize that it was for her that he had sacrificed his courage, as it was for her that he had sacrificed the sun and the air. This nervous sensibility had its drawbacks, no doubt—she was full of apologies when he flew at Mr Kenyon and bit him for stumbling over the bell-pull,* it was annoying when he moaned piteously all night because he was not allowed to sleep on her bed*—when he refused to eat unless she fed him; but she took the blame and bore the inconvenience because, after all, Flush loved her. He had refused the air and the sun for her sake. 'He is worth loving, is he not?'* she asked of Mr Horne. And whatever answer Mr Horne might give, Miss Barrett was positive of her own. She loved Flush, and Flush was worthy of her love.

It seemed as if nothing were to break that tie—as if the years were merely to compact and cement it; and as if those years were to be all the years of their natural lives. Eighteen-forty-two turned into eighteen-forty-three; eighteen-forty-three into eighteen-forty-four; eighteen-forty-four into eighteen-forty-five. Flush was no longer a puppy; he was a dog of four or five; he was a dog in the full prime of life—and still Miss Barrett lay on her sofa in Wimpole Street and still Flush lay on the sofa at her feet. Miss Barrett's life was the life of 'a bird in its cage'. She sometimes kept the house for weeks at a time, and when she left it, it was only for an hour or two, to drive to a shop in a carriage, or to be wheeled to Regent's

Park in a bath-chair. The Barretts never left London. Mr
Barrett, the seven brothers, the two sisters, the butler, Wilson
and the maids, Catiline, Folly, Miss Barrett and Flush all
went on living at 50 Wimpole Street, eating in the dining-
room, sleeping in the bedrooms, smoking in the study, cook-
ing in the kitchen, carrying hot-water cans and emptying the
slops from January to December. The chair-covers became
slightly soiled; the carpets slightly worn; coal dust, mud, soot,
fog, vapours of cigar smoke and wine and meat accumulated in
crevices, in cracks, in fabrics, on the tops of picture-frames, in
the scrolls of carvings. And the ivy that hung over Miss
Barrett's bedroom window flourished; its green curtain
became thicker and thicker, and in summer the nasturtiums
and the scarlet runners rioted together in the window-box.

But one night early in January 1845* the postman knocked.
Letters fell into the box as usual. Wilson went downstairs to
fetch the letters as usual. Everything was as usual—every
night the postman knocked, every night Wilson fetched the
letters, every night there was a letter for Miss Barrett. But
to-night the letter was not the same letter; it was a different
letter. Flush saw that, even before the envelope was broken.
He knew it from the way that Miss Barrett took it; turned it;
looked at the vigorous, jagged writing of her name. He knew it
from the indescribable tremor in her fingers, from the im-
petuosity with which they tore the flap open, from the
absorption with which she read. He watched her read. And as
she read he heard, as when we are half asleep we hear
through the clamour of the street some bell ringing and know
that it is addressed to us, alarmingly yet faintly, as if someone
far away were trying to rouse us with the warning of fire, or
burglary, or some menace against our peace and we start in

alarm before we wake—so Flush, as Miss Barrett read the little blotted sheet, heard a bell rousing him from his sleep; warning him of some danger; menacing his safety and bidding him sleep no more. Miss Barrett read the letter quickly; she read the letter slowly; she returned it carefully to its envelope. She too slept no more.

Again, a few nights later, there was the same letter on Wilson's tray. Again it was read quickly, read slowly, read over and over again. Then it was put away carefully, not in the drawer with the voluminous sheets of Miss Mitford's letters, but by itself. Now Flush paid the full price of long years of accumulated sensibility lying couched on cushions at Miss Barrett's feet. He could read signs that nobody else could even see. He could tell by the touch of Miss Barrett's fingers that she was waiting for one thing only—for the postman's knock, for the letter on the tray. She would be stroking him perhaps with a light, regular movement; suddenly—there was the rap—her fingers constricted; he would be held in a vice while Wilson came upstairs. Then she took the letter and he was loosed and forgotten.

Yet, he argued, what was there to be afraid of, so long as there was no change in Miss Barrett's life? And there was no change. No new visitors came. Mr Kenyon came as usual; Miss Mitford came as usual. The brothers and sisters came; and in the evening Mr Barrett came. They noticed nothing; they suspected nothing. So he would quieten himself and try to believe, when a few nights passed without the envelope, that the enemy had gone. A man in a cloak, he imagined, a cowled and hooded figure, had passed, like a burglar, rattling the door, and finding it guarded, had slunk away defeated. The danger, Flush tried to make himself believe, was over. The man had gone. And then the letter came again.

As the envelopes came more and more regularly, night after night, Flush began to notice signs of change in Miss Barrett herself. For the first time in Flush's experience she was irritable and restless. She could not read and she could not write. She stood at the window and looked out. She questioned Wilson anxiously about the weather—was the wind still in the east? Was there any sign of spring in the Park yet? Oh no, Wilson replied; the wind was a cruel east wind still. And Miss Barrett, Flush felt, was at once relieved and annoyed. She coughed. She complained of feeling ill—but not so ill as she usually felt when the wind was in the east. And then, when she was alone, she read over again last night's letter. It was the longest she had yet had. There were many pages, closely covered, darkly blotted, scattered with strange little abrupt hieroglyphics. So much Flush could see, from his station at her feet. But he could make no sense of the words that Miss Barrett was murmuring to herself. Only he could trace her agitation when she came to the end of the page and read aloud (though unintelligibly), 'Do you think I shall see you in two months, three months?'*

Then she took up her pen and passed it rapidly and nervously over sheet after sheet. But what did they mean —the little words that Miss Barrett wrote? 'April is coming. There will be both a May and a June if we live to see such things, and perhaps, after all, we may . . . I will indeed see you when the warm weather has revived me a little. . . . But I shall be afraid of you at first —though I am not, in writing thus. You are Paracelsus, and I am a recluse, with nerves that have been broken on the rack, and now hang loosely, quivering at a step and breath.'*

Flush could not read what she was writing an inch or two above his head. But he knew just as well as if he could read every word, how strangely his mistress was agitated as she wrote; what contrary desires shook her—that April might come; that April might not come; that she might see this unknown man at once, that she might never see him at all. Flush, too, quivered as she did at a step, at a breath. And remorselessly the days went on. The wind blew out the blind. The sun whitened the busts. A bird sang in the mews. Men went crying fresh flowers to sell down Wimpole Street. All these sounds meant, he knew, that April was coming and May and June—nothing could stop the approach of that dreadful spring. For what was coming with the spring? Some terror—some horror—something that Miss Barrett dreaded, and that Flush dreaded too. He started now at the sound of a step. But it was only Henrietta. Then there was a knock. It was only Mr Kenyon. So April passed; and the first twenty days of May. And then, on the 21st of May, Flush knew that the day itself had come. For on Tuesday, the 21st of May, Miss Barrett looked searchingly in the glass; arrayed herself exquisitely in her Indian shawls; bade Wilson draw the armchair close, but not too close; touched this, that and the other; and then sat upright among her pillows. Flush couched himself taut at her feet. They waited, alone together. At last, Marylebone Church clock struck two; they waited. Then Marylebone Church clock struck a single stroke—It was half-past two; and as the single stroke died away, a rap sounded boldly on the front door. Miss Barrett turned pale; she lay very still. Flush lay still too. Upstairs came the dreaded, the inexorable footfall; upstairs, Flush knew, came the cowled and sinister figure of midnight—the hooded man. Now his hand was on the door. The handle spun. There he stood.

'Mr Browning,' said Wilson.

Flush, watching Miss Barrett, saw the colour rush into her face; saw her eyes brighten and her lips open.

'Mr Browning!' she exclaimed.

Twisting his yellow gloves[3] in his hands, blinking his eyes, well groomed, masterly, abrupt, Mr Browning strode across the room. He seized Miss Barrett's hand, and sank into the chair by the sofa at her side. Instantly they began to talk.

What was horrible to Flush, as they talked, was his loneliness. Once he had felt that he and Miss Barrett were together, in a firelit cave. Now the cave was no longer firelit; it was dark and damp; Miss Barrett was outside. He looked round him. Everything had changed. The bookcase, the five busts—they were no longer friendly deities presiding approvingly—they were hostile, severe. He shifted his position at Miss Barrett's feet. She took no notice. He whined. They did not hear him. At last he lay still in tense and silent agony. The talk went on; but it did not flow and ripple as talk usually flowed and rippled. It leapt and jerked. It stopped and leapt again. Flush had never heard that sound in Miss Barrett's voice before—that vigour, that excitement. Her cheeks were bright as he had never seen them bright; her great eyes blazed as he had never seen them blaze. The clock struck four; and still they talked. Then it struck half-past four. At that Mr Browning jumped up. A horrid decision, a dreadful boldness marked every movement. In another moment he had wrung Miss Barrett's hand in his; he had taken his hat and gloves; he had said good-bye. They heard him running down the stairs. Smartly the door banged behind him. He was gone.

But Miss Barrett did not sink back in her pillows as she sank back when Mr Kenyon or Miss Mitford left her. Now she still sat upright; her eyes still burnt; her cheeks still glowed; she seemed still to feel that Mr Browning was with her. Flush touched her. She recalled him with a start. She patted him lightly, joyfully, on the head. And smiling, she gave him the oddest look—as if she wished that he could talk—as if she expected him too to feel what she felt. And then she laughed, pityingly; as if it were absurd—Flush, poor Flush could feel nothing of what she felt. He could know nothing of what she knew. Never had such wastes of dismal distance separated them. He lay there ignored; he might not have been there, he felt. Miss Barrett no longer remembered his existence.

And that night she ate her chicken to the bone. Not a scrap of potato or of skin was thrown to Flush. When Mr Barrett came as usual, Flush marvelled at his obtuseness. He sat himself down in the very chair that the man had sat in. His head pressed the same cushions that the man's had pressed, and yet he noticed nothing. 'Don't you know,' Flush marvelled, 'who's been sitting in that chair? Can't you smell him?' For to Flush the whole room still reeked of Mr Browning's presence. The air dashed past the bookcase, and eddied and curled round the heads of the five pale busts. But the heavy man sat by his daughter in entire self-absorption. He noticed nothing. He suspected nothing. Aghast at his obtuseness, Flush slipped past him out of the room.

But in spite of their astonishing blindness, even Miss Barrett's family began to notice, as the weeks passed, a change in Miss Barrett. She left her room and went down to sit in the drawing-room. Then she did what she had not done for many a long day—she actually walked on her own feet as far as the gate at Devonshire Place with her sister. Her friends, her family, were amazed at her improvement. But only Flush knew where her strength came from—it came from the dark man in the armchair. He came again and again and again. First it was once a week; then it was twice a week. He came always in the afternoon and left in the afternoon. Miss Barrett always saw him alone. And on the days when he did not come, his letters came. And when he himself was gone, his flowers were there. And in the mornings when she was alone, Miss Barrett wrote to him. That dark, taut, abrupt, vigorous man, with his black hair, his red cheeks and his yellow gloves, was everywhere. Naturally, Miss Barrett was better; of course she could walk. Flush himself felt that it was impossible to lie still. Old longings revived; a new restlessness possessed him. Even his sleep was full of dreams. He dreamt as he had not dreamt since the old days at Three Mile Cross—of hares starting from the long grass; of pheasants rocketing up with long tails streaming, of partridges rising with a whirr from the stubble. He dreamt that he was hunting, that he was chasing some spotted spaniel, who fled, who escaped him. He was in Spain; he was in Wales; he was in Berkshire; he was flying before park-keepers' truncheons in Regent's Park. Then he opened his eyes. There were no hares, and no partridges; no whips cracking and no black men crying 'Span! Span!' There was only Mr Browning in the armchair talking to Miss Barrett on the sofa.

Sleep became impossible while that man was there. Flush lay with his eyes wide open, listening. Though he could make no sense of the little words that hurled over his head from two-thirty to four-thirty sometimes three times a week, he could detect with terrible accuracy that the tone of the words was changing. Miss Barrett's voice had been forced and unnaturally lively at first. Now it had gained a warmth and an ease that he had never heard in it before. And every time the man came, some new sound came into their voices—now they made a grotesque chattering; now they skimmed over him like birds flying widely; now they cooed and clucked, as if they were two birds settled in a nest; and then Miss Barrett's voice, rising again, went soaring and circling in the air; and then Mr Browning's voice barked out its sharp, harsh clapper of laughter; and then there was only a murmur, a quiet humming sound as the voices joined together. But as the summer turned to autumn Flush noted, with horrid apprehension, another note. There was a new urgency, a new pressure and energy in the man's voice, at which Miss Barrett, Flush felt, took fright. Her voice fluttered; hesitated; seemed to falter and fade and plead and gasp, as if she were begging for a rest, for a pause, as if she were afraid. Then the man was silent.

Of him they took but little notice. He might have been a log of wood lying there at Miss Barrett's feet for all the attention Mr Browning paid him. Sometimes he scrubbed his head in a brisk, spasmodic way, energetically, without sentiment, as he passed him. Whatever that scrub might mean, Flush felt nothing but an intense dislike for Mr Browning. The very sight of him, so well tailored, so tight, so muscular, screwing his yellow gloves in his hand, set his teeth on edge. Oh! to let them meet sharply, completely in the stuff of his trousers! And yet he dared not. Taking it all in all, that winter—1845–6—was the most distressing that Flush had ever known.

The winter passed; and spring came round again. Flush could see no end to the affair; and yet just as a river, though it reflects still trees and grazing cows and rooks returning to the tree-tops, moves inevitably to a waterfall, so those days, Flush knew, were moving to catastrophe. Rumours of change hovered in the air. Sometimes he thought that some vast exodus impended. There was that indefinable stir in the house which precedes—could it be possible?—a journey. Boxes were actually dusted, were, incredible as it might seem, opened. Then they were shut again. No, it was not the family that was going to move. The brothers and sisters still went in and out as usual. Mr Barrett paid his nightly visit, after the man had gone, at his accustomed hour. What was it, then, that was going to happen? for as the summer of 1846 wore on, Flush was positive that a change was coming. He could hear it again in the altered sound of the eternal voices. Miss Barrett's voice, that had been pleading and afraid, lost its faltering note. It rang out with a determination and a boldness that Flush had never heard in it before. If only Mr Barrett could hear the tone in which she welcomed this usurper, the laugh with which she greeted him, the exclamation with which he took her hand in his! But nobody was in the room with them except Flush. To him the change was of the most galling nature. It was not merely that Miss Barrett was changing towards Mr Browning—she was changing in every relation—in her feeling towards Flush himself. She treated his advances more brusquely; she cut short his endearments laughingly; she made him feel that there was something petty, silly, affected, in his old affectionate ways. His vanity was exacerbated. His jealousy was inflamed. At last, when July came, he determined to make one violent attempt to regain her favour, and perhaps to oust the newcomer. How to accomplish this double purpose he did not know, and could not plan. But suddenly on the 8th of July his feelings overcame him. He flung himself on Mr Browning and bit him savagely. At last his teeth met in the immaculate cloth of Mr Browning's trousers! But the limb inside was hard as iron—Mr Kenyon's leg had been butter in comparison. Mr Browning brushed him off with a flick of his hand and went on talking. Neither he nor Miss Barrett seemed to think the attack worthy of attention. Completely foiled, worsted, without a shaft left in his sheath, Flush sank back on his cushions panting with rage and disappointment. But he had misjudged Miss Barrett's insight. When Mr Browning was gone, she called him to her and inflicted upon him the worst punishment he had ever known. First she slapped his ears—that was nothing; oddly enough the slap was rather to his liking; he would have welcomed another. But then she said in her sober, certain tones that she would never love him again. That shaft went to his heart. All these years they had lived together, shared everything together, and now, for one moment's failure, she would never love him again. Then, as if to make her dismissal complete, she took the flowers that Mr Browning had brought her and began to put them in water in a vase. It was an act, Flush thought, of calculated and deliberate malice; an act designed to make him feel his own insignificance completely. 'This rose is from him,' she seemed to say, 'and this carnation. Let the red shine by the yellow; and the yellow by the red. And let the green leaf lie there—' And, setting one flower with another, she stood back to gaze at them as if he were before her—the man in the yellow gloves—a mass of brilliant flowers. But even so, even as she pressed the leaves and flowers together, she could not altogether ignore the fixity with which Flush gazed at her. She could not deny that 'expression of quite despair on his face'. She could not but relent. 'At last I said, "If you are good, Flush, you may come and say that you are sorry", on which he

[43]

dashed across the room and, trembling all over, kissed first one of my hands and then another, and put up his paws to be shaken, and looked into my face with such beseeching eyes that you would certainly have forgiven him just as I did.'* That was her account of the matter to Mr Browning; and he of course replied: 'Oh, poor Flush, do you think I do not love and respect him for his jealous supervision—his slowness to know another, having once known you?'* It was easy enough for Mr Browning to be magnanimous, but that easy magnanimity was perhaps the sharpest thorn that pressed into Flush's side.

Another incident a few days later showed how widely they were separated, who had been so close, how little Flush could now count on Miss Barrett for sympathy. After Mr Browning had gone one afternoon Miss Barrett decided to drive to Regent's Park with her sister. As they got out at the Park gate the door of the four-wheeler shut on Flush's paw. He 'cried piteously' and held it up to Miss Barrett for sympathy. In other days sympathy in abundance would have been lavished upon him for less. But now a detached, a mocking, a critical expression came into her eyes. She laughed at him. She thought he was shamming: '. . . no sooner had he touched the grass than he began to run without a thought of it',* she wrote. And she commented sarcastically, 'Flush always makes the most of his misfortunes—he is of the Byronic school—*il se pose en victime*'* But here Miss Barrett, absorbed in her own emotions, misjudged him completely. If his paw had been broken, still he would have bounded. That dash was his answer to her mockery; I have done with you—that was the meaning he flashed at her as he ran. The flowers smelt bitter to him; the grass burnt his paws; the dust filled his nostrils with disillusion. But he raced—he scampered. 'Dogs must be led on chains'—there was the usual placard; there were the park-keepers with their top-hats and their truncheons to enforce it. But 'must' no longer had any meaning for him. The chain of love was broken. He would run where he liked; chase partridges; chase spaniels; splash into the middle of dahlia beds; break brilliant, blowing red and yellow roses. Let the park-keepers throw their truncheons if they chose. Let them dash his brains out. Let him fall dead, disembowelled, at Miss Barrett's feet. He cared nothing. But naturally nothing of the kind happened. Nobody pursued him; nobody noticed him. The solitary park-keeper was talking to a nursemaid. At last he returned to Miss Barrett and she absent-mindedly slipped the chain over his neck, and led him home.

After two such humiliations the spirit of an ordinary dog, the spirit even of an ordinary human being, might well have been broken. But Flush, for all his softness and silkiness, had eyes that blazed; had passions that leapt not merely in bright flame but sunk and smouldered. He resolved to meet his enemy face to face and alone. No third person should interrupt this final conflict. It should be fought out by the principals themselves. On the afternoon of Tuesday, the 21st of July, therefore, he slipped downstairs and waited in the hall. He had not long to wait. Soon he heard the tramp of the familiar footstep in the street; he heard the familiar rap on the door. Mr Browning was admitted. Vaguely aware of the impending attack and determined to meet it in the most conciliatory of spirits, Mr Browning had come provided with a parcel of cakes. There was Flush waiting in the hall. Mr Browning made, evidently, some well-meant attempt to caress him; perhaps he even went so far as to offer him a cake. The gesture was enough. Flush sprang upon his enemy with unparalleled violence. His teeth once more met in Mr Browning's trousers. But unfortunately in the excitement of the moment he forgot what was most essential—silence. He barked; he flung himself on Mr Browning, barking loudly. The sound was sufficient to alarm the household. Wilson rushed downstairs. Wilson beat him soundly. Wilson overpowered him completely. Wilson led him in ignominy away. Ignominy it was—to have attacked Mr Browning, to have been beaten by Wilson. Mr Browning had not lifted a finger. Taking his cakes with him, Mr Browning proceeded unhurt, unmoved, in perfect composure, upstairs, alone to the bedroom. Flush was led away.

After two and a half hours of miserable confinement with parrots and beetles, ferns and saucepans, in the kitchen, Flush was summoned to Miss Barrett's presence. She was lying on the sofa with her sister Arabella beside her. Conscious of the rightness of his cause, Flush went straight to her. But she refused to look at him. He turned to Arabella. She merely said, 'Naughty Flush, go away'. Wilson was there—the formidable, the implacable Wilson. It was to her that Miss Barrett turned for information. She had beaten him, Wilson said, 'because it was right'. And, she added, she had only beaten him with her hand. It was upon her evidence that Flush was convicted. The attack, Miss Barrett assumed, had been unprovoked; she credited Mr Browning with all virtue, with all generosity; Flush had been beaten off by a servant, without a whip, because 'it was right'. There was no more to be said. Miss Barrett decided against him. 'So he lay down on the floor at my feet,' she wrote, 'looking from under his eyebrows at me.'* But though Flush might look, Miss Barrett refused even to meet his eyes. There she lay on the sofa; there Flush lay on the floor.

And as he lay there, exiled, on the carpet, he went through one of those whirlpools of tumultuous emotion in which the soul is either dashed upon the rocks and splintered or, finding some tuft of foothold, slowly and painfully pulls itself up, regains dry land, and at last emerges on top of a ruined universe to survey a world created afresh on a different plan. Which was it to be—destruction or reconstruction? That was the question. The outlines only of his dilemma can be traced here; for his debate was silent. Twice Flush had done his utmost to kill his enemy; twice he had failed. And why had he failed, he asked himself? Because he loved Miss Barrett. Looking up at her from under his eyebrows as she lay, severe and silent on the sofa, he knew that he must love her for ever. Things are not simple but complex. If he bit Mr Browning he bit her too. Hatred is not hatred; hatred is also love. Here Flush shook his ears in an agony of perplexity. He turned uneasily on the floor. Mr Browning was Miss Barrett—Miss Barrett was Mr Browning; love is hatred and hatred is love. He stretched himself, whined and raised his head from the floor. The clock struck eight. For three hours or more he had been lying there, tossed from the horn of one dilemma to another.

Even Miss Barrett, severe, cold, implacable as she was, laid down her pen. 'Wicked Flush!' she had been writing to Mr Browning, '. . . if people like Flush, choose to behave like dogs savagely, they must take the consequences indeed, as dogs usually do! And *you*, so good and gentle to him! Anyone but *you* would have said "hasty words" at least.'* Really it would be a good plan, she thought, to buy a muzzle. And then she looked up and saw Flush. Something unusual in his look must have struck her. She paused. She laid down her pen.

[47]

Once he had roused her with a kiss, and she had thought that he was Pan. He had eaten chicken and rice pudding soaked in cream. He had given up the sunshine for her sake. She called him to her and said she forgave him.

But to be forgiven, as if for a passing whim, to be taken back again on the sofa as if he had learnt nothing in his anguish on the floor, as if he were the same dog when in fact he differed totally, was impossible. For the moment, exhausted as he was, Flush submitted. A few days later, however, a remarkable scene took place between him and Miss Barrett which showed the depths of his emotions. Mr Browning had been and gone; Flush was alone with Miss Barrett. Normally he would have leapt on to the sofa at her feet. But now, instead of jumping up as usual and claiming her caress, Flush went to what was now called 'Mr Browning's armchair'. Usually the chair was abhorrent to him; it still held the shape of his enemy. But now, such was the battle he had won, such was the charity that suffused him, that he not only looked at the chair, but, as he looked, 'suddenly fell into a rapture'. Miss Barrett, watching him intently, observed this extraordinary portent. Next she saw him turn his eyes towards a table. On that table still lay the packet of Mr Browning's cakes. He 'reminded me that the cakes you left were on the table'.* They were now old cakes, stale cakes, cakes bereft of any carnal seduction. Flush's meaning was plain. He had refused to eat the cakes when they were fresh, because they were offered by an enemy. He would eat them now that they were stale, because they were offered by an enemy turned to friend, because they were symbols of hatred turned to love. Yes, he signified, he would eat them now. So Miss Barrett rose and took the cakes in her hand. And as she gave them to him she admonished him, 'So I explained to him that *you* had brought them for him, and that he ought to be properly ashamed therefore for his past wickedness, and make up his mind to love you and not bite you for the future—and he was allowed to profit from your goodness to him'.* As he swallowed down the faded flakes of that distasteful pastry—it was mouldy, it was fly-blown, it was sour—Flush solemnly repeated, in his own language, the words she had used—he swore to love Mr Browning and not bite him for the future.

He was instantly rewarded—not by stale cakes, not by chicken's wings, not by the caresses that were now his, nor by the permission to lie once more on the sofa at Miss Barrett's feet. He was rewarded, spiritually; yet the effects were curiously physical. Like an iron bar corroding and festering and killing all natural life beneath it, hatred had lain all these months across his soul. Now, by the cutting of sharp knives and painful surgery, the iron had been excised. Now the blood ran once more; the nerves shot and tingled; flesh formed; Nature rejoiced, as in spring. Flush heard the birds sing again; he felt the leaves growing on the trees; as he lay on the sofa at Miss Barrett's feet, glory and delight coursed through his veins. He was with them, not against them, now; their hopes, their wishes, their desires were his. Flush could have barked in sympathy with Mr Browning now. The short, sharp words raised the hackles on his neck. 'I need a week of Tuesdays,' Mr Browning cried, 'then a month—a year—a life!'* I, Flush echoed him, need a month—a year—a life! I need all the things that you both need. We are all three conspirators in the most glorious of causes. We are joined in sympathy. We are joined in hatred. We are joined in defiance of black and beetling tyranny. We are joined in love.—In short, all Flush's hopes now were set upon some dimly apprehended but none the less certainly emerging triumph, upon some glorious victory that was to be theirs in common, when suddenly, without a word of warning, in the midst of civilization, security and friendship—he was in a shop in Vere Street* with Miss Barrett and her sister: it was the morning of Tuesday the 12th of September*—Flush was tumbled head over heels into darkness. The doors of a dungeon shut upon him. He was stolen.[4]

CHAPTER IV

WHITECHAPEL

'THIS morning Arabel and I, and he with us,' Miss Barrett wrote, 'went in a cab to Vere Street where we had a little business, and he followed us as usual into a shop and out of it again, and was at my heels when I stepped up into the carriage. Having turned, I said "Flush", and Arabel looked round for Flush—there was no Flush! He had been caught up in that moment, from *under* the wheels, do you understand?'* Mr Browning understood perfectly well. Miss Barrett had forgotten the chain; therefore Flush was stolen. Such, in the year 1846, was the law of Wimpole Street and its neighbourhood.

Nothing, it is true, could exceed the apparent solidity and security of Wimpole Street itself. As far as an invalid could walk or a bath-chair could trundle nothing met the eye but an agreeable prospect of four-storeyed houses, plate-glass windows and mahogany doors. Even a carriage and pair, in the course of an afternoon's airing, need not, if the coachman were discreet, leave the limits of decorum and respectability. But if you were not an invalid, if you did not possess a carriage and pair, if you were—and many people were—active and able-bodied and fond of walking, then you might see sights and hear language and smell smells, not a stone's-throw from Wimpole Street, that threw doubts upon the solidity even of Wimpole Street itself. So Mr Thomas Beames* found when about this time he took it into his head to go walking about

London. He was surprised; indeed he was shocked. Splendid
buildings raised themselves in Westminster, yet just behind
them were ruined sheds in which human beings lived herded
together above herds of cows—'two in each seven feet of
space'.* He felt that he ought to tell people what he had seen.
Yet how could one describe politely a bedroom in which two
or three families lived above a cow-shed, when the cow-shed
had no ventilation, when the cows were milked and killed and
eaten under the bedroom? That was a task, as Mr Beames
found when he came to attempt it, that taxed all the resources
of the English language. And yet he felt that he ought to
describe what he had seen in the course of an afternoon's walk
through some of the most aristocratic parishes in London.
The risk of typhus was so great. The rich could not know what
dangers they were running. He could not altogether hold his
tongue when he found what he did find at Westminster and
Paddington and Marylebone. For instance, here was an old
mansion formerly belonging to some great nobleman. Relics
of marble mantelpieces remained. The rooms were panelled
and the banisters were carved, and yet the floors were rotten,
the walls dripped with filth; hordes of half-naked men and
women had taken up their lodging in the old banqueting-halls.
Then he walked on. Here an enterprising builder had pulled
down the old family mansion. He had run up a jerry-built
tenement house in its place. The rain dripped through the
roof and the wind blew through the walls. He saw a child
dipping a can into a bright-green stream and asked if they
drank that water. Yes, and washed in it too, for the landlord
only allowed water to be turned on twice a week. Such sights
were the more surprising, because one might come upon them
in the most sedate and civilized quarters of London—'the

most aristocratic parishes have their share'.* Behind Miss Barrett's bedroom, for instance, was one of the worst slums in London. Mixed up with that respectability was this squalor. But there were certain quarters, of course, which had long been given over to the poor and were left undisturbed. In Whitechapel, or in a triangular space of ground at the bottom of the Tottenham Court Road, poverty and vice and misery had bred and seethed and propagated their kind for centuries without interference. A dense mass of aged buildings in St Giles's was 'wellnigh a penal settlement, a pauper metropolis in itself'.* Aptly enough, where the poor conglomerated thus, the settlement was called a Rookery. For there human beings swarmed on top of each other as rooks swarm and blacken tree-tops. Only the buildings here were not trees; they were hardly any longer buildings. They were cells of brick intersected by lanes which ran with filth. All day the lanes buzzed with half-dressed human beings; at night there poured back again into the stream the thieves, beggars and prostitutes who had been plying their trade all day in the West End. The police could do nothing. No single wayfarer could do anything except hurry through as fast as he could and perhaps drop a hint, as Mr Beames did, with many quotations, evasions and euphemisms, that all was not quite as it should be. Cholera would come, and perhaps the hint that cholera would give would not be quite so evasive.

But in the summer of 1846 that hint had not yet been given; and the only safe course for those who lived in Wimpole Street and its neighbourhood was to keep strictly within the respectable area and to lead your dog on a chain. If one forgot, as Miss Barrett forgot, one paid the penalty, as Miss Barrett was now to pay it. The terms upon which Wimpole Street lived cheek by jowl with St Giles's were well known. St Giles's stole what St Giles's could; Wimpole Street paid what Wimpole Street must. Thus Arabel at once 'began to comfort me by showing how certain it was that I should recover him for ten pounds at most'.* Ten pounds, it was reckoned, was about the price that Mr Taylor would ask for a cocker spaniel. Mr Taylor was the head of the gang. As soon as a lady in Wimpole Street lost her dog she went to Mr Taylor; he named his price, and it was paid; or if not, a brown paper parcel was delivered in Wimpole Street a few days later containing the head and paws of the dog. Such, at least, had been the experience of a lady in the neighbourhood who had tried to make terms with Mr Taylor. But Miss Barrett of course intended to pay. Therefore when she got home she told her brother Henry, and Henry went to see Mr Taylor that afternoon. He found him 'smoking a cigar in a room with pictures'*—Mr Taylor was said to make an income of two or three thousand a year out of the dogs of Wimpole Street—and Mr Taylor promised that he would confer with his 'Society' and that the dog would be returned next day. Vexatious as it was, and especially annoying at a moment when Miss Barrett needed all her money, such were the inevitable consequences of forgetting in 1846 to keep one's dog on a chain.

But for Flush things were very different. Flush, Miss Barrett reflected, 'doesn't know that we can recover him'; Flush had never mastered the principles of human society. 'All this night he will howl and lament, I know perfectly',* Miss Barrett wrote to Mr Browning on the afternoon of Tuesday, the 2nd September. But while Miss Barrett wrote to Mr Browning, Flush was going through the most terrible experience of his life. He was bewildered in the extreme. One moment he was in Vere Street, among ribbons and laces; the next he was tumbled head over heels into a bag; jolted rapidly across streets, and at length was tumbled out—here. He found himself in complete darkness. He found himself in chillness and dampness. As his giddiness left him he made out a few shapes in a low dark room—broken chairs, a tumbled mattress. Then he was seized and tied tightly by the leg to some obstacle. Something sprawled on the floor—whether beast or human being, he could not tell. Great boots and draggled skirts kept stumbling in and out. Flies buzzed on scraps of old meat that were decaying on the floor. Children crawled out from dark corners and pinched his ears. He whined, and a heavy hand beat him over the head. He cowered down on the few inches of damp brick against the wall. Now he could see that the floor was crowded with animals of different kinds. Dogs tore and worried a festering bone that they had got between them. Their ribs stood out from their coats—they were half famished, dirty, diseased, uncombed, unbrushed; yet all of them, Flush could see, were dogs of the highest breeding, chained dogs, footmen's dogs, like himself.

He lay, not daring even to whimper, hour after hour. Thirst was his worst suffering; but one sip of the thick greenish water that stood in a pail near him disgusted him; he would rather die than drink another. Yet a majestic greyhound was drinking greedily. Whenever the door was kicked open he looked up. Miss Barrett—was it Miss Barrett? Had she come at last? But it was only a hairy ruffian, who kicked them all aside and stumbled to a broken chair upon which he flung himself. Then gradually the darkness thickened. He could scarcely make out what shapes those were, on the floor, on the mattress, on the broken chairs. A stump of candle was stuck on the ledge over the fireplace. A flare burnt in the gutter outside. By its flickering, coarse light Flush could see terrible faces passing outside, leering at the window. Then in they came, until the small crowded room became so crowded that he had to shrink back and lie even closer against the wall. These horrible monsters—some were ragged, others were flaring with paint and feathers—squatted on the floor; hunched themselves over the table. They began to drink; they cursed and struck each other. Out tumbled, from the bags that were dropped on the floor, more dogs—lapdogs, setters, pointers, with their collars still on them; and a giant cockatoo that flustered and fluttered its way from corner to corner shrieking 'Pretty Poll', 'Pretty Poll', with an accent that would have terrified its mistress, a widow in Maida Vale. Then the women's bags were opened, and out were tossed on to the table bracelets and rings and brooches such as Flush had seen Miss Barrett wear and Miss Henrietta. The demons pawed and clawed them; cursed and quarrelled over them. The dogs barked. The children shrieked, and the splendid cockatoo— such a bird as Flush had often seen pendant in a Wimpole Street window—shrieked 'Pretty Poll! Pretty Poll!' faster and faster until a slipper was thrown at it and it flapped its great yellow-stained dove-grey wings in frenzy. Then the candle toppled over and fell. The room was dark. It grew steadily hotter and hotter; the smell, the heat, were unbearable, Flush's nose burnt; his coat twitched. And still Miss Barrett did not come.

Miss Barrett lay on her sofa in Wimpole Street. She was vexed; she was worried, but she was not seriously alarmed. Of course Flush would suffer; he would whine and bark all night; but it was only a question of a few hours. Mr Taylor would name his sum; she would pay it; Flush would be returned.

The morning of Wednesday the 3rd September dawned in the rookeries of Whitechapel. The broken windows gradually became smeared with grey. Light fell upon the hairy faces of ruffians lying sprawled upon the floor. Flush woke from a trance that had veiled his eyes and once more realized the truth. This was now the truth—this room, these ruffians, these whining, snapping, tightly tethered dogs, this murk, this dampness. Could it be true that he had been in a shop, with ladies, among ribbons, only yesterday? Was there such a place as Wimpole Street? Was there a room where fresh water sparkled in a purple jar; had he lain on cushions; had he been given a chicken's wing nicely roasted; and had he been torn with rage and jealousy and bitten a man with yellow gloves? The whole of that life and its emotions floated away, dissolved, became unreal.

Here, as the dusty light filtered in, a woman heaved herself off a sack and staggered out to fetch beer. The drinking and the cursing began again. A fat woman held him up by his ears and pinched his ribs, and some odious joke was made about him—there was a roar of laughter as she threw him on the floor again. The door was kicked open and banged to. Whenever that happened he looked up. Was it Wilson? Could it possibly be Mr Browning? Or Miss Barrett? But no—it was only another thief, another murderer; he cowered back at the mere sight of those draggled skirts, of those hard, horny boots. Once he tried to gnaw a bone that was hurled his way. But his teeth could not meet in stony flesh and the rank smell disgusted him. His thirst increased and he was forced to lap a little of the green water that had been spilt from the pail. But as Wednesday wore on and he became hotter and more parched and still more sore, lying on the broken boards, one thing merged in another. He scarcely noticed what was happening. It was only when the door opened that he raised his head and looked. No, it was not Miss Barrett.

Miss Barrett, lying on the sofa in Wimpole Street, was becoming anxious. There was some hitch in the proceedings. Taylor had promised that he would go down to Whitechapel on Wednesday afternoon and confer with 'the Society'. Yet Wednesday afternoon, Wednesday evening passed and still Taylor did not come. This could only mean, she supposed, that the price was going to be raised—which was inconvenient enough at the moment. Still, of course, she would have to pay it. 'I must have my Flush, you know,' she wrote to Mr Browning. 'I can't run any risk and bargain and haggle.'* So she lay on the sofa writing to Mr Browning and listening for a knock at the door. But Wilson came up with the letters; Wilson came up with the hot water. It was time for bed and Flush had not come.

Thursday the 4th of September dawned in Whitechapel. The door opened and shut. The red setter who had been whining all night beside Flush on the floor was hauled off by a ruffian in a moleskin vest—to what fate? Was it better to be killed or to stay here? Which was worse—this life or that death? The racket, the hunger and the thirst, the reeking smells of the place—and once, Flush remembered, he had detested the scent of eau-de-Cologne—were fast obliterating any clear image, any single desire. Fragments of old memories began turning in his head. Was that the voice of old Dr Mitford shouting in the field? Was that Kerenhappock gossiping with the baker at the door? There was a rattling in the room and he thought he heard Miss Mitford tying up a bunch of geraniums. But it was only the wind—for it was stormy to-day—battering at the brown paper in the broken window pane. It was only some drunken voice raving in the gutter. It was only the old hag in the corner mumbling on and on and on as she fried a herring in a pan over a fire. He had been forgotten and deserted. No help was coming. No voice spoke to him—the parrots cried 'Pretty Poll, Pretty Poll', and the canaries kept up their senseless cheeping and chirping.

Then again evening darkened the room; the candle was stuck in its saucer; the coarse light flared outside; hordes of sinister men with bags on their backs, of garish women with painted faces, began to shuffle in at the door and to fling themselves down on the broken beds and tables. Another night had folded its blackness over Whitechapel. And the rain dripped steadily through a hole in the roof and drummed into a pail that had been stood to catch it. Miss Barrett had not come.

Thursday dawned in Wimpole Street. There was no sign of Flush—no message from Taylor. Miss Barrett was very much alarmed. She made enquiries. She summoned her brother Henry, and cross-examined him. She found out that he had tricked her. 'The archfiend' Taylor had come according to his promise the night before. He had stated his terms—six guineas for the Society and half a guinea for himself. But Henry, instead of telling her, had told Mr Barrett, with the result, of course, that Mr Barrett had ordered him not to pay, and to conceal the visit from his sister. Miss Barrett was 'very vexed and angry'. She bade her brother to go at once to Mr Taylor and pay the money. Henry refused and 'talked of Papa'. But it was no use talking of Papa, she protested. While they talked of Papa, Flush would be killed. She made up her mind. If Henry would not go, she would go herself: '. . . if people won't do as I choose, I shall go down to-morrow morning, and bring Flush back with me',* she wrote to Mr Browning.

But Miss Barrett now found that it was easier to say this than to do it. It was almost as difficult for her to go to Flush as for Flush to come to her. All Wimpole Street was against her. The news that Flush was stolen and that Taylor demanded a ransom was now public property. Wimpole Street was determined to make a stand against Whitechapel. Blind Mr Boyd sent word that in his opinion it would be 'an awful sin' to pay the ransom. Her father and her brother were in league against her and were capable of any treachery in the interests of their class. But worst of all—far worse—Mr Browning himself threw all his weight, all his eloquence, all his learning, all his logic, on the side of Wimpole Street and against Flush. If Miss Barrett gave way to Taylor, he wrote, she was giving way to tyranny; she was giving way to blackmailers; she was increasing the power of evil over right, of wickedness over innocence. If she gave Taylor his demand, '. . . how will the poor owners fare who have not money enough for their dogs' redemption'? His imagination took fire; he imagined what he would say if Taylor asked him even for five shillings; he would say, '*You* are responsible for the proceedings of your gang, and *you* I mark—don't talk nonsense to me about cutting off heads or paws. Be as sure as that I stand here and tell you, I will spend my whole life in putting you down, the nuisance you declare yourself—and by every imaginable means I will be the death of you and as many of your accomplices as I can discover—but *you* I have discovered and will never lose sight of . . .'* So Mr

Browning would have replied to Taylor if he had had the good fortune to meet that gentleman. For indeed, he went on, catching a later post with a second letter that same Thursday afternoon, '. . . it is horrible to fancy how all the oppressors in their several ranks may, if they choose, twitch back to them by the heartstrings after various modes the weak and silent whose secret they have found out'.* He did not blame Miss Barrett —nothing she did could be anything but perfectly right, perfectly acceptable to him. Still, he continued on Friday morning, 'I think it lamentable weakness . . .'* If she encouraged Taylor who stole dogs, she encouraged Mr Barnard Gregory* who stole characters. Indirectly, she was responsible for all the wretches who cut their throats or fly the country because some blackmailer like Barnard Gregory took down a directory and blasted their characters. 'But why write all this string of truisms about the plainest thing in the world?'* So Mr Browning stormed and vociferated from New Cross twice daily.

Lying on her sofa, Miss Barrett read the letters. How easy it would have been to yield—how easy it would have been to say, 'Your good opinion is worth more to me than a hundred cocker spaniels'. How easy it would have been to sink back on her pillows and sigh, 'I am a weak woman; I know nothing of law and justice; decide for me'. She had only to refuse to pay the ransom; she had only to defy Taylor and his Society. And if Flush were killed, if the dreadful parcel came and she opened it and out dropped his head and paws, there was Robert Browning by her side to assure her that she had done right and earned his respect. But Miss Barrett was not to be intimidated. Miss Barrett took up her pen and refuted Robert Browning. It was all very well, she said, to quote Donne;* to cite the case of Gregory; to invent spirited replies to Mr Taylor—she would have done the same had Taylor struck her; had Gregory defamed her;—would that they had! But what would Mr Browning have done if the banditti had stolen her; had *her* in their power; threatened to cut off *her* ears and send them by post to New Cross? Whatever he would have done, her mind was made up. Flush was helpless. Her duty was to him. 'But Flush, poor Flush, who has loved me so faithfully; have I a right to sacrifice *him* in his innocence, for the sake of any Mr Taylor's guilt in the world?'* Whatever Mr Browning might say, she was going to rescue Flush, even if she went down into the jaws of Whitechapel to fetch him, even if Robert Browning despised her for doing so.

On Saturday, therefore, with Mr Browning's letter lying open on the table before her, she began to dress. She read his 'one word more—in all this, I labour against the execrable policy of the world's husbands, fathers, brothers and domineerers in general'.* So, if she went to Whitechapel she was siding against Robert Browning, and in favour of fathers, brothers and domineerers in general. Still, she went on dressing. A dog howled in the mews. It was tied up, helpless in the power of cruel men. It seemed to her to cry as it howled: 'Think of Flush'.* She put on her shoes, her cloak, her hat. She glanced at Mr Browning's letter once more. 'I am about to marry you',* she read. Still the dog howled. She left her room and went downstairs.

Henry Barrett met her and told her that in his opinion she might well be robbed and murdered if she did what she threatened. She told Wilson to call a cab. All trembling but submissive, Wilson obeyed. The cab came. Miss Barrett told Wilson to get in. Wilson, though convinced that death awaited her, got in. Miss Barrett told the cabman to drive to Manning Street, Shoreditch.* Miss Barrett got in herself and off they drove. Soon they were beyond plate-glass windows, the mahogany doors and the area railings. They were in a world that Miss Barrett had never seen, had never guessed at. They were in a world where cows are herded under bedroom floors, where whole families sleep in rooms with broken windows; in a world where water is turned on only twice a week, in a world where vice and poverty breed vice and poverty. They had come to a region unknown to respectable cab-drivers. The cab stopped; the driver asked his way at a public-house. 'Out came two or three men. "Oh, you want to find Mr Taylor, I daresay!"' In this mysterious world a cab with two ladies could only come upon one errand, and that errand was already known. It was sinister in the extreme. One of the men ran into a house, and came out saying that Mr Taylor '"wasn't at home! but wouldn't I get out?" Wilson, in an aside of terror, entreated me not to think of such a thing.' A gang of men and boys pressed round the cab. 'Then wouldn't I see Mrs Taylor?' the man asked. Miss Barrett had no wish whatever to see Mrs Taylor; but now an immense fat woman came out of the house, 'fat enough to have had an easy conscience all her life', and informed Miss Barrett that her husband was out: 'might be in in a few minutes, or in so many hours—wouldn't I like to get out and wait?' Wilson tugged at her gown. Imagine waiting in the house of that woman! It was bad enough to sit in the cab with the gang of men and boys pressing round them. So Miss Barrett parleyed with the 'immense feminine bandit' from the cab. Mr Taylor had her dog, she said; Mr Taylor had promised to restore her dog; would Mr Taylor bring back her dog to Wimpole Street for certain that very day? 'Oh yes, certainly,' said the fat woman with the most gracious of smiles. She did believe that Taylor had left home precisely on that business. And she 'poised her head to right and left with the most easy grace'.

So the cab turned round and left Manning Street, Shoreditch. Wilson was of the opinion that 'we had escaped with our lives barely'. Miss Barrett herself had been alarmed. 'Plain enough it was that the gang was strong there. The Society, the "Fancy" . . . had their roots in the ground', she wrote. Her mind teemed with thoughts, her eyes were full of pictures. This, then, was what lay on the other side of Wimpole Street—these faces, these houses. She had seen more while she sat in the cab at the public-house than she had seen during the five years that she had lain in the back bedroom at Wimpole Street. 'The faces of those men!'* she exclaimed. They were branded on her eyeballs. They stimulated her imagination as 'the divine marble presences', the busts on the bookcase, had never stimulated it. Here lived women like herself; while she lay on her sofa, reading, writing, they lived thus. But the cab was now trundling along between four-storeyed houses again. Here was the familiar avenue of doors and windows: the pointed brick, the brass knockers, the regular curtains. Here was Wimpole Street and No. 50. Wilson sprang out—with what relief to find herself in safety can be imagined. But Miss Barrett perhaps hesitated a moment. She still saw 'the faces of those men'. They were to come before her again years later when she sat writing on a sunny balcony in Italy.[5] They were to inspire the most vivid passages in *Aurora Leigh*.* But now the butler had opened the door, and she went upstairs to her room again.

Saturday was the fifth day of Flush's imprisonment.

Almost exhausted, almost hopeless, he lay panting in his dark corner of the teeming floor. Doors slammed and banged. Rough voices cried. Women screamed. Parrots chattered as they had never chattered to widows in Maida Vale, but now evil old women merely cursed at them. Insects crawled in his fur, but he was too weak, too indifferent to shake his coat. All Flush's past life and its many scenes—Reading, the greenhouse, Miss Mitford, Mr Kenyon, the bookcases, the busts, the peasants on the blind—had faded like snowflakes dissolved in a cauldron. If he still held to hope, it was to something nameless and formless; the featureless face of someone he still called 'Miss Barrett'. She still existed; all the rest of the world was gone; but she still existed, though such gulfs lay between them that it was impossible, almost, that she should reach him still. Darkness began to fall again, such darkness as seemed almost able to crush out his last hope—Miss Barrett.

In truth, the forces of Wimpole Street were still, even at this last moment, battling to keep Flush and Miss Barrett apart. On Saturday afternoon she lay and waited for Taylor to come, as the immensely fat woman had promised. At last he came, but he had not brought the dog. He sent up a message —Let Miss Barrett pay him six guineas on the spot, and he would go straight to Whitechapel and fetch the dog 'on his word of honour'. What 'the archfiend' Taylor's word of honour might be worth, Miss Barrett could not say; but 'there seemed no other way for it'; Flush's life was at stake; she counted out the guineas and sent them down to Taylor in the passage. But as ill luck would have it, as Taylor waited in the passage among the umbrellas, the engravings, the pile carpet and other valuable objects, Alfred Barrett came in. The sight of the archfiend actually in the house made him lose his temper. He burst into a rage. He called him 'a swindler, and a liar and a thief'. Thereupon Mr Taylor cursed him back. What was far worse, he swore that 'as he hoped to be saved, we should never see our dog again', and rushed out of the house. Next morning, then, the bloodstained parcel would arrive.

Miss Barrett flung on her clothes again and rushed downstairs. Where was Wilson? Let her call a cab. She was going back to Shoreditch instantly. Her family came running to prevent her. It was getting dark. She was exhausted already. The adventure was risky enough for a man in health. For her it was madness. So they told her. Her brothers, her sisters, all came round her threatening her, dissuading her, 'crying out against me for being "quite mad" and obstinate and wilful—I was called as many names as Mr Taylor'. But she stood her ground. At last they realized the extent of her folly. Whatever the risk might be they must give way to her. Septimus promised if Ba would return to her room 'and be in good humour'* he would go to Taylor's himself and pay the money and bring back the dog.

So the dusk of the 5th of September faded into the blackness of night in Whitechapel. The door of the room was once more kicked open. A hairy man hauled Flush by the scruff of his neck out of his corner. Looking up into the hideous face of his old enemy, Flush did not know whether he was being taken to be killed or to be freed. Save for one phantom memory, he did not care. The man stooped. What were those great fingers fumbling at his throat for? Was it a knife or a chain? Stumbling, half blinded, on legs that staggered, Flush was led out into the open air.

In Wimpole Street Miss Barrett could not eat her dinner.

Was Flush dead, or was Flush alive? She did not know. At eight o'clock there was a rap on the door; it was the usual letter from Mr Browning. But as the door opened to admit the letter, something rushed in also;—Flush. He made straight for his purple jar. It was filled three times over; and still he drank. Miss Barrett watched the dazed, bewildered dirty dog, drinking. 'He was not so enthusiastic about seeing me as I expected',* she remarked. No, there was only one thing in the world he wanted—clean water.

After all, Miss Barrett had but glanced at the faces of those men and she remembered them all her life. Flush had been at their mercy in their midst for five whole days. Now as he lay on cushions once more, cold water was the only thing that seemed to have any substance, any reality. He drank continually. The old gods of the bedroom—the bookcase, the wardrobe, the busts—seemed to have lost their substance. This room was no longer the whole world; it was only a shelter. It was only a dell arched over by one trembling dock-leaf in a forest where wild beasts prowled and venomous snakes coiled; where behind every tree lurked a murderer ready to pounce. As he lay dazed and exhausted on the sofa at Miss Barrett's feet the howls of tethered dogs, the screams of birds in terror still sounded in his ears. When the door opened he started, expecting a hairy man with a knife—it was only Mr Kenyon with a book; it was only Mr Browning with his yellow gloves. But he shrank away from Mr Kenyon and Mr Browning now. He trusted them no longer. Behind those smiling, friendly faces was treachery and cruelty and deceit. Their caresses were hollow. He dreaded even walking with Wilson to the pillar-box. He would not stir without his chain. When they said, 'Poor Flush, did the naughty men take you away?'

he put up his head and moaned and yelled. A whip cracking sent him bolting down the area-steps into safety. Indoors he crept closer to Miss Barrett on the sofa. She alone had not deserted him. He still kept some faith in her. Gradually some substance returned to her. Exhausted, trembling, dirty and very thin, he lay on the sofa at her feet.

As the days passed and the memory of Whitechapel grew fainter, Flush, lying close to Miss Barrett on the sofa, read her feelings more clearly than ever before. They had been parted; now they were together. Indeed they had never been so much akin. Every start she gave, every movement she made, passed through him too. And she seemed now to be perpetually starting and moving. The delivery of a parcel even made her jump. She opened the parcel; with trembling fingers she took out a pair of thick boots. She hid them instantly in the corner of the cupboard. Then she lay down as if nothing had happened; yet something had happened. When they were alone she rose and took a diamond necklace from a drawer. She took out the box that held Mr Browning's letters. She laid the boots, the necklace and the letters all in a carpet-box together and then—as if she heard a step on the stair—she pushed the box under the bed and lay down hastily, covering herself with her shawl again. Such signs of secrecy and stealth must herald, Flush felt, some approaching crisis. Were they about to fly together? Were they about to escape together from this awful world of dog-stealers and tyrants? Oh that it were possible! He trembled and whined with excitement; but in her low voice Miss Barrett bade him be quiet, and instantly he was quiet. She was very quiet too. She lay perfectly still on the sofa directly any of her brothers or sisters came in; she lay and talked to Mr Barrett as she always lay and talked to Mr Barrett.

But on Saturday, the 12th of September, Miss Barrett did what Flush had never known her do before. She dressed herself as if to go out directly after breakfast. Moreover, as he watched her dress, Flush knew perfectly well from the expression on her face that he was not to go with her. She was bound on secret business of her own. At ten Wilson came into the room. She also was dressed as if for a walk. They went out together; and Flush lay on the sofa and waited for their return. An hour or so later Miss Barrett came back alone. She did not look at him—she seemed to look at nothing. She drew off her gloves and for a moment he saw a gold band shine on one of the fingers of her left hand. Then he saw her slip the ring from her hand and hide it in the darkness of a drawer. Then she laid herself down as usual on the sofa. He lay by her side scarcely daring to breathe, for whatever had happened, it was something that must at all costs be concealed.

At all costs the life of the bedroom must go on as usual. Yet everything was different. The very movement of the blind as it drew in and out seemed to Flush like a signal. And as the lights and shadows passed over the busts they too seemed to be hinting and beckoning. Everything in the room seemed to be aware of change; to be prepared for some event. And yet all was silent; all was concealed. The brothers and sisters came in and out as usual; Mr Barrett came as usual in the evening. He looked as usual to see that the chop was finished, the wine drunk. Miss Barrett talked and laughed and gave no sign when anyone was in the room that she was hiding anything. Yet when they were alone she pulled out the box from under the bed and filled it hastily, stealthily, listening as she did so. And the signs of strain were unmistakable. On Sunday the church bells were ringing. 'What bells are those?' somebody asked.

'Marylebone Church bells', said Miss Henrietta. Miss Barrett, Flush saw, went deadly white. But nobody else seemed to notice anything.

So Monday passed, and Tuesday and Wednesday and Thursday. Over them all lay a blanket of silence, of eating and talking and lying still on the sofa as usual. Flush, tossing in uneasy sleep, dreamt that they were couched together under ferns and leaves in the darkness, in a vast forest; then the leaves were parted and he woke. It was dark; but he saw Wilson come stealthily into the room, and take the box from beneath the bed and quietly carry it outside. This was on Friday night, the 19th of September. All Saturday morning he lay as one lies who knows that at any moment now a hand-kerchief may drop, a low whistle may sound and the signal will be given for death or for life. He watched Miss Barrett dress herself. At a quarter to four the door opened and Wilson came in. Then the signal was given—Miss Barrett lifted him in her arms. She rose and walked to the door. For a moment they stood looking round the room. There was the sofa and by it Mr Browning's armchair. There were the busts and the tables. The sun filtered through the ivy leaves and the blind with peasants walking blew gently out. All was as usual. All seemed to expect a million more such movements to come to them; but to Miss Barrett and Flush this was the last. Very quietly Miss Barrett shut the door.

Very quietly they slipped downstairs, past the drawing-room, the library, the dining-room. All looked as they usually looked; smelt as they usually smelt; all were quiet as if sleeping in the hot September afternoon. On the mat in the hall Catiline lay sleeping too. They gained the front door and very quietly turned the handle. A cab was waiting outside.

'To Hodgson's',* said Miss Barrett. She spoke almost in a whisper. Flush sat on her knee very still. Not for anything in the whole world would he have broken that tremendous silence.

CHAPTER V

ITALY

HOURS, days, weeks, it seemed of darkness and rattling; of sudden lights; and then long tunnels of gloom; of being flung this way and that; of being hastily lifted into the light and seeing Miss Barrett's face close, and thin trees and lines and rails and high light-specked houses—for it was the barbarous custom of railways in those days to make dogs travel in boxes—followed.* Yet Flush was not afraid; they were escaping; they were leaving tyrants and dog-stealers behind them. Rattle, grind; grind, rattle as much as you like, he murmured, as the train flung him this way and that; only let us leave Wimpole Street and Whitechapel behind us. At last the light broadened; the rattling stopped. He heard birds singing and the sigh of trees in the wind. Or was it the rush of water? Opening his eyes at last, shaking his coat at last, he saw—the most astonishing sight conceivable. There was Miss Barrett on a rock in the midst of rushing waters. Trees bent over her; the river raced round her. She must be in peril. With one bound Flush splashed through the stream and reached her. '. . . he is baptized in Petrarch's name', said Miss Barrett as he clambered up on to the rock by her side. For they were at Vaucluse;* she had perched herself upon a stone in the middle of Petrarch's fountain.

Then there was more rattling and more grinding; and then again he was stood down on a stable floor; the darkness opened; light poured over him; he found himself alive, awake, bewildered, standing on reddish tiles in a vast bare room flooded with sunshine. He ran hither and thither smelling and touching. There was no carpet and no fireplace. There were no sofas, no armchairs, no bookcases, no busts. Pungent and unfamiliar smells tickled his nostrils and made him sneeze. The light, infinitely sharp and clear, dazzled his eyes. He had never been in a room—if this were indeed a room—that was so hard, so bright, so big, so empty. Miss Barrett looked smaller than ever sitting on a chair by a table in the midst. Then Wilson took him out of doors. He found himself almost blinded, first by the sun, then by the shadow. One half of the street was burning hot; the other bitterly cold. Women went by wrapped in furs, yet they carried parasols to shade their heads. And the street was dry as bone. Though it was now the middle of November there was neither mud nor puddle to wet his paws or clot their feathers. There were no areas and no railings. There was none of that heady confusion of smells that made a walk down Wimpole Street or Oxford Street so distracting. On the other hand, the strange new smells that came from sharp stone corners, from dry yellow walls, were extraordinarily pungent and queer. Then from behind a black swinging curtain came an astonishing sweet smell, wafted in clouds; he stopped, his paws raised, to savour it; he made to follow it inside; he pushed in beneath the curtain. He had one glimpse of a booming light-sprinkled hall, very high and hollow; and then Wilson with a cry of horror, jerked him smartly back. They went on down the street again. The noise of the street was deafening. Everybody seemed to be shouting shrilly at the same moment. Instead of the solid and soporific hum of London there was a rattling and a crying, a jingling and a shouting, a cracking of whips and a jangling of bells.

Flush leapt and jumped this way and that, and so did Wilson. They were forced on and off the pavement twenty times, to avoid a cart, a bullock, a troop of soldiers, a drove of goats. He felt younger, spryer than he had done these many years. Dazzled, yet exhilarated, he sank on the reddish tiles and slept more soundly than he had ever slept in the back bedroom at Wimpole Street upon pillows.

But soon Flush became aware of the more profound differences that distinguish Pisa*—for it was in Pisa that they were now settled—from London. The dogs were different. In London he could scarcely trot round to the pillar-box without meeting some pug dog, retriever, bulldog, mastiff, collie, Newfoundland, St Bernard, fox terrier or one of the seven famous families of the Spaniel tribe. To each he gave a different name, and to each a different rank. But here in Pisa, though dogs abounded, there were no ranks; all—could it be possible?—were mongrels. As far as he could see, they were dogs merely—grey dogs, yellow dogs, brindled dogs, spotted dogs; but it was impossible to detect a single spaniel, collie, retriever or mastiff among them. Had the Kennel Club,* then, no jurisdiction in Italy? Was the Spaniel Club unknown? Was there no law which decreed death to the topknot, which cherished the curled ear, protected the feathered foot, and insisted absolutely that the brow must be domed but not pointed? Apparently not. Flush felt himself like a prince in exile. He was the sole aristocrat among a crowd of *canaille*.* He was the only pure-bred cocker spaniel in the whole of Pisa.

For many years now Flush had been taught to consider himself an aristocrat. The law of the purple jar and of the chain had sunk deep into his soul. It is scarcely surprising that he was thrown off his balance. A Howard or a Cavendish set down among a swarm of natives in mud huts can hardly be blamed if now and again he remembers Chatsworth* and muses regretfully over red carpets and galleries daubed with coronets as the sunset blazes down through painted windows. There was an element, it must be admitted, of the snob in Flush; Miss Mitford had detected it years ago; and the sentiment, subdued in London among equals and superiors, returned to him now that he felt himself unique. He became overbearing and impudent. 'Flush has grown an absolute monarch and barks one distracted when he wants a door opened', Mrs Browning wrote. 'Robert', she continued, 'declares that the said Flush considers him, my husband, to be created for the especial purpose of doing him service, and really it looks rather like it.'*

'Robert', 'my husband'—if Flush had changed, so had Miss Barrett. It was not merely that she called herself Mrs Browning now; that she flashed the gold ring on her hand in the sun; she was changed, as much as Flush was changed. Flush heard her say 'Robert', 'my husband', fifty times a day, and always with a ring of pride that made his hackles rise and his heart jump. But it was not her language only that had changed. She was a different person altogether. Now, for instance, instead of sipping a thimbleful of port and complaining of the headache, she tossed off a tumbler of Chianti and slept the sounder. There was a flowering branch of oranges on the dinner-table instead of one denuded, sour, yellow fruit. Then instead of driving in a barouche landau* to Regent's Park she pulled on her thick boots and scrambled over rocks. Instead of sitting in a carriage and rumbling along Oxford Street, they rattled off in a ramshackle fly* to the borders of a lake and looked at mountains; and when she was tired she did

not hail another cab; she sat on a stone and watched the
lizards. She delighted in the sun; she delighted in the cold.
She threw pine logs from the Duke's forest on to the fire if it
froze. They sat together in the crackling blaze and snuffed up
the sharp, aromatic scent. She was never tired of praising Italy
at the expense of England. '. . . our poor English', she exclaimed, 'want educating into gladness. They want refining
not in the fire but in the sunshine.' Here in Italy was freedom
and life and the joy that the sun breeds. One never saw men
fighting, or heard them swearing; one never saw the Italians
drunk;—'the faces of those men' in Shoreditch came again
before her eyes. She was always comparing Pisa with London
and saying how much she preferred Pisa. In the streets of Pisa
pretty women could walk alone; great ladies first emptied
their own slops and then went to Court 'in a blaze of
undeniable glory'.* Pisa with all its bells, its mongrels, its
camels, its pine woods, was infinitely preferable to Wimpole
Street and its mahogany doors and its shoulders of mutton. So
Mrs Browning every day, as she tossed off her Chianti and
broke another orange from the branch, praised Italy and
lamented poor, dull, damp, sunless, joyless, expensive, conventional England.

Wilson, it is true, for a time maintained her British balance.
The memory of butlers and basements, of front doors and
curtains, was not obliterated from her mind without an effort.
She still had the conscience to walk out of a picture gallery
'struck back by the indecency of the Venus'.* And later, when
she was allowed, by the kindness of a friend, to peep through a
door at the glories of the Grand Ducal Court,* she still loyally
upheld the superior glory of St James's. 'It . . . was all very
shabby', she reported, 'in comparison with our English

Court.'* But even as she gazed, the superb figure of one of the Grand Duke's bodyguard caught her eye. Her fancy was fired; her judgement reeled; her standards toppled. Lily Wilson fell passionately in love with Signor Righi,* the guardsman.[6]

And just as Mrs Browning was exploring her new freedom and delighting in the discoveries she made, so Flush too was making his discoveries and exploring his freedom. Before they left Pisa—in the spring of 1847 they moved on to Florence*—Flush had faced the curious and at first upsetting truth that the laws of the Kennel Club are not universal. He had brought himself to face the fact that light topknots are not necessarily fatal. He had revised his code accordingly. He had acted, at first with some hesitation, upon his new conception of canine society. He was becoming daily more and more democratic. Even in Pisa, Mrs Browning noticed, '. . . he goes out every day and speaks Italian to the little dogs'.* Now in Florence the last threads of his old fetters fell from him. The moment of liberation came one day in the Cascine.* As he raced over the grass 'like emeralds' with 'the pheasants all alive and flying',* Flush suddenly bethought him of Regent's Park and its proclamation: Dogs must be led on chains. Where was 'must' now? Where were chains now? Where were park-keepers and truncheons? Gone, with the dog-stealers and Kennel Clubs and Spaniel Clubs of a corrupt aristocracy! Gone with four-wheelers and hansom cabs! with Whitechapel and Shoreditch! He ran, he raced; his coat flashed; his eyes blazed. He was the friend of all the world now. All dogs were his brothers. He had no need of a chain in this new world; he had no need of protection. If Mr Browning was late in going for his walk—he and Flush were the best of friends now —Flush boldly summoned him. He 'stands up before him and barks in the most imperious manner possible',* Mrs Browning observed with some irritation—for her relations with Flush were far less emotional now than in the old days; she no longer needed his red fur and his bright eyes to give her what her own experience lacked; she had found Pan for herself among the vineyards and the olive trees; he was there too beside the pine fire of an evening. So if Mr Browning loitered, Flush stood up and barked; but if Mr Browning preferred to stay at home and write, it did not matter. Flush was independent now. The wistarias and the laburnum were flowering over walls; the judas trees were burning bright in the gardens; the wild tulips were sprinkled in the fields. Why should he wait? Off he ran by himself. He was his own master now. '. . . he goes out by himself, and stays hours together', Mrs Browning wrote; '. . . knows every street in Florence—will have his own way in everything. I am never frightened at his absence',* she added, remembering with a smile those hours of agony in Wimpole Street and the gang waiting to snatch him up under the horses' feet if she forgot his chain in Vere Street. Fear was unknown in Florence; there were no dog-stealers here and, she may have sighed, there were no fathers.

But, to speak candidly, it was not to stare at pictures, to penetrate into dark churches and look up at dim frescoes, that Flush scampered off when the door of Casa Guidi was left open. It was to enjoy something, it was in search of something denied him all these years. Once the hunting horn of Venus had blown its wild music over the Berkshire fields; he had loved Mr Partridge's dog; she had borne him a child. Now he heard the same voice pealing down the narrow streets of Florence, but more imperiously, more impetuously, after all these years of silence. Now Flush knew what men can never

know—love pure, love simple, love entire; love that brings
train of care in its wake; that has no shame; no remorse; that is
here, that is gone, as the bee on the flower is here and is gone.
To-day the flower is a rose, to-morrow a lily; now it is the wild
thistle on the moor, now the pouched and portentous orchid
of the conservatory. So variously, so carelessly Flush em-
braced the spotted spaniel down the alley, and the brindled
dog and the yellow dog—it did not matter which. To Flush it
was all the same. He followed the horn wherever the horn
blew and the wind wafted it. Love was all; love was enough.
No one blamed him for his escapades. Mr Browning merely
laughed—'Quite disgraceful for a respectable dog like
him'*—when Flush returned very late at night or early the
next morning. And Mrs Browning laughed too, as Flush flung
himself down on the bedroom floor and slept soundly upon
the arms of the Guidi family inlaid in scagliola.*

For at Casa Guidi the rooms were bare. All those draped
objects of his cloistered and secluded days had vanished. The
bed was a bed; the wash-stand was a wash-stand. Everything
was itself and not another thing. The drawing-room was large
and sprinkled with a few old carved chairs of ebony. Over the
fire hung a mirror with two cupids to hold the lights. Mrs
Browning herself had discarded her Indian shawls. She wore a
cap made of some thin bright silk that her husband liked. Her
hair was brushed in a new way. And when the sun had gone
down and the shutters had been raised she paced the balcony
dressed in thin white muslin. She loved to sit there looking,
listening, watching the people in the street.

They had not been long in Florence before one night there
was such a shouting and trampling in the street* that they ran
to the balcony to see what was happening. A vast crowd was

surging underneath. They were carrying banners and shouting and singing. All the windows were full of faces; all the
balconies were full of figures. The people in the windows were
tossing flowers and laurel leaves on to the people in the street;
and the people in the street—grave men, gay young women
—were kissing each other and raising their babies to the
people in the balconies. Mr and Mrs Browning leant over the
balustrade and clapped and clapped. Banner after banner
passed. The torches flashed their light on them. 'Liberty' was
written on one; 'The Union of Italy' on another; and 'The
Memory of the Martyrs' and 'Viva Pio Nono'* and 'Viva
Leopoldo Secondo'—for three and a half hours the banners
went by and the people cheered and Mr and Mrs Browning
stood with six candles burning on the balcony, waving and
waving. For some time Flush too, stretched between them
with his paws over the sill, did his best to rejoice. But at
last—he could not conceal it—he yawned. 'He confessed at
last that he thought they were rather long about it',* Mrs
Browning observed. A weariness, a doubt, a ribaldry
possessed him. What was it all for? he asked himself. Who was
this Grand Duke and what had he promised? Why were they
all so absurdly excited?—for the ardour of Mrs Browning,
waving and waving, as the banners passed, somehow annoyed
him. Such enthusiasm for a Grand Duke was somehow
exaggerated, he felt. And then, as the Grand Duke passed, he
became aware that a little dog had stopped at the door. Seizing
his chance when Mrs Browning was more than usually
enthusiastic, he slipped down from the balcony and made off.
Through the banners and the crowds he followed her. She
fled further and further into the heart of Florence. Far away
sounded the shouting; the cheers of the people died down into

silence. The lights of the torches were extinguished. Only a star or two shone in the ripples of the Arno where Flush lay with the spotted spaniel* by his side, couched in the shell of an old basket on the mud. There tranced in love they lay till the sun rose in the sky. Flush did not return until nine next morning, and Mrs Browning greeted him rather ironically— he might at least, she thought, have remembered that it was the first anniversary of her wedding day. But she supposed 'he had been very much amused'.* It was true. While she had found an inexplicable satisfaction in the trampling of forty thousand people, in the promises of Grand Dukes and the windy aspirations of banners, Flush infinitely preferred the little dog at the door.

It cannot be doubted that Mrs Browning and Flush were reaching different conclusions in their voyages of discovery —she a Grand Duke, he a spotted spaniel;—and yet the tie which bound them together was undeniably still binding. No sooner had Flush abolished 'must' and raced free through the emerald grass of the Cascine gardens where the pheasants fluttered red and gold, than he felt a check. Once more he was thrown back on his haunches. At first it was nothing—a hint merely—only that Mrs Browning in the spring of 1849 became busy with her needle.* And yet there was something in the sight that gave Flush pause. She was not used to sew. He noted that Wilson moved a bed and that she opened a drawer to put white clothes inside it. Raising his head from the tiled floor, he looked, he listened attentively. Was something once more about to happen? He looked anxiously for signs of trunks and packing. Was there to be another flight, another escape? But an escape to what, from what? There is nothing to be afraid of here, he assured Mrs Browning. They need neither of them worry themselves in Florence about Mr Taylor and dogs' heads wrapped up in brown paper parcels. Yet he was puzzled. The signs of change, as he read them, did not signify escape. They signified, much more mysteriously, expectance. Something, he felt, as he watched Mrs Browning so composedly, yet silently and steadfastly, stitching in her low chair, was coming that was inevitable; yet to be dreaded. As the weeks went on, Mrs Browning scarcely left the house. She seemed, as she sat there, to anticipate some tremendous event. Was she about to encounter somebody, like the ruffian Taylor, and let him rain blows on her alone and unaided? Flush quivered with apprehension at the thought. Certainly she had no intention of running away. No boxes were packed. There was no sign that anybody was about to leave the house—rather there were signs that somebody was coming. In his jealous anxiety Flush scrutinized each new-comer. There were many now—Miss Blagden, Mr Landor, Hattie Hosmer, Mr Lytton*—ever so many ladies and gentlemen now came to Casa Guidi. Day after day Mrs Browning sat there in her armchair quietly stitching.

Then one day early in March Mrs Browning did not appear in the sitting-room at all. Other people came in and out; Mr Browning and Wilson came in and out; and they came in and out so distractedly that Flush hid himself under the sofa. People were trampling up and down stairs, running and calling in low whispers and muted unfamiliar voices. They were moving upstairs in the bedroom. He crept further and further under the shadow of the sofa. He knew in every fibre of his body that some change was taking place—some awful event was happening. So he had waited, years ago, for the step of the hooded man on the staircase. And at last the door had opened and Miss Barrett had cried 'Mr Browning!' Who was coming now? What hooded man? As the day wore on, he was left completely alone; nobody came into the drawing-room. He lay in the drawing-room without food or drink; a thousand spotted spaniels might have sniffed at the door and he would have shrunk away from them. For as the hours passed he had an overwhelming sense that something was thrusting its way into the house from outside. He peeped out from beneath the flounces. The cupids holding the lights, the ebony chests, the French chairs, all looked thrust asunder; he himself felt as if he were being pushed up against the wall to make room for something he could not see. Once he saw Mr Browning; once Wilson, but she was changed too—as if they were both seeing the invisible presence that he felt. Their eyes were oddly glazed.

At last Wilson, looking very flushed and untidy but triumphant, took him in her arms and carried him upstairs. They entered the bedroom. There was a faint bleating in the shadowed room—something waved on the pillow. It was a live animal. Independently of them all, without the street door being opened, out of herself in the room, alone, Mrs Browning had become two people. The horrid thing waved and mewed by her side. Torn with rage and jealousy and some deep disgust that he could not hide, Flush struggled himself free and rushed downstairs. Wilson and Mrs Browning called him back; they tempted him with caresses; they offered him titbits; but it was useless. He cowered away from the disgusting sight, the repulsive presence, wherever there was a shadowy sofa or a dark corner. '. . . for a whole fortnight he fell into deep melancholy and was proof against all attentions lavished on him'*—so Mrs Browning, in the midst of all her other distractions, was forced to notice. And when we take, as we must, human minutes and hours and drop them into a dog's mind and see how the minutes swell into hours and the hours into days, we shall not exaggerate if we conclude that Flush's 'deep melancholy' lasted six full months by the human clock. Many men and women have forgotten their hates and their loves in less.

But Flush was no longer the unschooled, untrained dog of Wimpole Street days. He had learnt his lesson. Wilson had struck him. He had been forced to swallow cakes that were stale when he might have eaten them fresh; he had sworn to love and not to bite. All this churned in his mind as he lay under the sofa; and at last he issued out. Again he was rewarded. At first, it must be admitted, the reward was insubstantial if not positively disagreeable. The baby was set on his back and Flush had to trot about with the baby pulling his ears. But he submitted with such grace, only turning round, when his ears were pulled, 'to kiss the little bare, dimpled feet', that, before three months had passed, this helpless, weak, puling, muling lump had somehow come to prefer him, 'on the whole'*—so Mrs Browning said—to other people. And then, strangely enough, Flush found that he returned the baby's affection. Did they not share something in common—did not the baby somehow resemble Flush in many ways? Did they not hold the same views, the same tastes? For instance, in the matter of scenery. To Flush all scenery was insipid. He had never, all these years, learnt to focus his eyes upon mountains. When they took him to Vallombrosa* all the splendours of its woods had merely bored him. Now again, when the baby was a few months old, they went on another of those long expeditions in a travelling carriage. The baby lay on his nurse's lap; Flush sat on Mrs Browning's knee. The carriage went on and on and on, painfully climbing the heights of the Apennines. Mrs Browning was almost beside herself with delight. She could scarcely tear herself from the window. She could not find words enough in the whole of the English language to express what she felt. '. . . the exquisite, almost visionary scenery of the Apennines, the wonderful variety of shape and colour, the sudden transitions and vital individuality of those mountains, the chestnut forests dropping by their own weight into the deep ravines, the rocks cloven and clawed by the living torrents, and the hills, hill above hill, piling up their grand existences as if they did it themselves, changing colour in the effort'—the beauty of the Apennines brought words to birth in such numbers that they positively crushed each other out of existence. But the baby and Flush felt none of this stimulus, none of this inadequacy. Both were silent. Flush drew 'in his head from the window and didn't consider it worth looking at . . . He has a supreme contempt for trees and hills or anything of that kind', Mrs Browning concluded. The carriage rumbled on. Flush slept and the baby slept. Then at last there were lights and houses and men and women passing the windows. They had entered a village. Instantly Flush was all attention. '. . . his eyes were starting out of his head with eagerness; he looked east, he looked west, you would conclude that he was taking notes or preparing them.'* It was the human scene that stirred him. Beauty, so it seems at least, had to be crystallized into a green or violet powder and puffed by some celestial syringe down the fringed channels that lay behind his nostrils before it touched Flush's senses; and then it issued not in words, but in a silent rapture. Where Mrs Browning saw, he smelt; where she wrote, he snuffed.

Here, then, the biographer must perforce come to a pause. Where two or three thousand words are insufficient for what we see—and Mrs Browning had to admit herself beaten by the Apennines: 'Of these things I cannot give you any idea',* she admitted—there are no more than two words and one-half for what we smell. The human nose is practically non-existent. The greatest poets in the world have smelt nothing but roses on the one hand, and dung on the other. The infinite gradations that lie between are unrecorded. Yet it was in the world of smell that Flush mostly lived. Love was chiefly smell; form and colour were smell; music and architecture, law, politics and science were smell. To him religion itself was smell. To describe his simplest experience with the daily chop or biscuit is beyond our power. Not even Mr Swinburne* could have said what the smell of Wimpole Street meant to Flush on a hot afternoon in June. As for describing the smell of a spaniel mixed with the smell of torches, laurels, incense, banners, wax candles and a garland of rose leaves crushed by a satin heel that has been laid up in camphor, perhaps Shake-speare, had he paused in the middle of writing *Antony and Cleopatra*—But Shakespeare did not pause. Confessing our inadequacy, then, we can but note that to Flush Italy, in these the fullest, the freest, the happiest years of his life, meant mainly a succession of smells. Love, it must be supposed, was gradually losing its appeal. Smell remained. Now that they were established in Casa Guidi again, all had their avocations. Mr Browning wrote regularly in one room; Mrs Browning wrote regularly in another. The baby played in the nursery. But Flush wandered off into the streets of Florence to enjoy the rapture of smell. He threaded his path through main streets and back streets, through squares and alleys, by smell.

He nosed his way from smell to smell; the rough, the smooth, the dark, the golden. He went in and out, up and down, where they beat brass, where they bake bread, where the women sit combing their hair, where the bird-cages are piled high on the causeway, where the wine spills itself in dark red stains on the pavement, where leather smells and harness and garlic, where cloth is beaten, where vine leaves tremble, where men sit and drink and spit and dice—he ran in and out, always with his nose to the ground, drinking in the essence; or with his nose in the air vibrating with the aroma. He slept in this hot patch of sun—how sun made the stone reek! he sought that tunnel of shade—how acid shade made the stone smell! He devoured whole bunches of ripe grapes largely because of their purple smell; he chewed and spat out whatever tough relic of goat or macaroni the Italian housewife had thrown from the balcony —goat and macaroni were raucous smells, crimson smells. He followed the swooning sweetness of incense into the violet intricacies of dark cathedrals; and, sniffing, tried to lap the gold on the window-stained tomb. Nor was his sense of touch much less acute. He knew Florence in its marmoreal smoothness and in its gritty and cobbled roughness. Hoary folds of drapery, smooth fingers and feet of stone received the lick of his tongue, the quiver of his shivering snout. Upon the infinitely sensitive pads of his feet he took the clear stamp of proud Latin inscriptions. In short, he knew Florence as no human being has ever known it; as Ruskin* never knew it or George Eliot* either. He knew it as only the dumb know. Not a single one of his myriad sensations ever submitted itself to the deformity of words.

But though it would be pleasant for the biographer to infer that Flush's life in the late middle age was an orgy of pleasure transcending all description; to maintain that while the baby day by day picked up a new word and thus removed sensation a little further beyond reach, Flush was fated to remain for ever in a Paradise where essences exist in their utmost purity, and the naked soul of things presses on the naked nerve—it would not be true. Flush lived in no such Paradise. The spirit, ranging from star to star, the bird whose furthest flight over polar snows or tropical forests never brings it within sight of human houses and their curling wood-smoke, may, for anything we know, enjoy such immunity, such integrity of bliss. But Flush had lain upon human knees and heard men's voices. His flesh was veined with human passions; he knew all grades of jealousy, anger and despair. Now in summer he was scourged by fleas.[7] With a cruel irony the sun that ripened the grapes brought also the fleas. '. . . Savonarola's martyrdom here in Florence', wrote Mrs Browning, 'is scarcely worse than Flush's in the summer.'* Fleas leapt to life in every corner of the Florentine houses; they skipped and hopped out of every cranny of the old stone; out of every fold of old tapestry; out of every cloak, hat and blanket. They nested in Flush's fur. They bit their way into the thickest of his coat. He scratched and tore. His health suffered; he became morose, thin and feverish. Miss Mitford was appealed to. What remedy was there, Mrs Browning wrote anxiously, for fleas?* Miss Mitford, still sitting in her greenhouse at Three Mile Cross, still writing tragedies, put down her pen and looked up her old prescriptions—what Mayflower had taken, what Rosebud. But the fleas of Reading die at a pinch. The fleas of Florence are red and virile. To them Miss Mitford's powders might well have been snuff. In despair Mr and Mrs Browning went down on their knees beside a pail of water and did their best to exorcise the pest with soap and scrubbing-brush. It was in vain. At last one day Mr Browning, taking Flush for a walk, noticed that people pointed; he heard a man lay a finger to his nose and whisper 'La rogna' (mange). As by this time 'Robert is as fond of Flush as I am',* to take his walk of an afternoon with a friend and to hear him thus stigmatized was intolerable. Robert, his wife wrote, 'wouldn't bear it any longer'. Only one remedy remained, but it was a remedy that was almost as drastic as the disease itself. However democratic Flush had become and careless of the signs of rank, he still remained what Philip Sidney had called him, a gentleman by birth. He carried his pedigree on his back. His coat meant to him what a gold watch inscribed with the family arms means to an impoverished squire whose broad acres have shrunk to that single circle. It was the coat that Mr Browning now proposed to sacrifice. He called Flush to him and, 'taking a pair of scissors, clipped him all over into the likeness of a lion'.*

As Robert Browning snipped, as the insignia of a cocker spaniel fell to the floor, as the travesty of quite a different animal rose round his neck, Flush felt himself emasculated, diminished, ashamed. What am I now? he thought, gazing into the glass. And the glass replied with the brutal sincerity of glasses, 'You are nothing'. He was nobody. Certainly he was no longer a cocker spaniel. But as he gazed, his ears bald now, and uncurled, seemed to twitch. It was as if the potent spirits of truth and laughter were whispering in them. To be nothing—is that not, after all, the most satisfactory state in the whole world? He looked again. There was his ruff. To caricature the pomposity of those who claim that they are something—was that not in its way a career? Anyhow, settle the matter as he might, there could be no doubt that he was free from fleas. He shook his ruff. He danced on his nude, attenuated legs. His spirits rose. So might a great beauty, rising from a bed of sickness and finding her face eternally disfigured, make a bonfire of clothes and cosmetics, and laugh with joy to think that she need never look in the glass again or dread a lover's coolness or a rival's beauty. So might a clergyman, cased for twenty years in starch and broadcloth, cast his collar into the dustbin and snatch the works of Voltaire* from the cupboard. So Flush scampered off clipped all over into the likeness of a lion, but free from fleas. 'Flush,' Mrs Browning wrote to her sister, 'is wise.'* She was thinking perhaps of the Greeks saying that happiness is only to be reached through suffering. The true philosopher is he who has lost his coat but is free from fleas.

But Flush had not long to wait before his newly won philosophy was put to the test. Again in the summer of 1852* there were signs at Casa Guidi of one of those crises which, gathering soundlessly as a drawer opens or as a piece of string is left dangling from a box, are to a dog as menacing as the clouds which foretell lightning to a shepherd or as the rumours which foretell war to a statesman. Another change was indicated, another journey. Well, what of that? Trunks were hauled down and corded. The baby was carried out in his nurse's arms. Mr and Mrs Browning appeared, dressed for travelling. There was a cab at the door. Flush waited philosophically in the hall. When they were ready he was ready. Now that they were all seated in the carriage, with one bound Flush sprang lightly in after them. To Venice, to Rome, to Paris—where were they going? All countries were equal to him now; all men were his brothers. He had learnt that lesson for himself. But when finally he emerged from obscurity he had need of all his philosophy—he was in London.

Houses spread to right and left in sharp avenues of regular brick. The pavement was cold and hard beneath his feet. And there, issuing from a mahogany door with a brass knocker, was a lady bountifully apparelled in flowing robes of purple plush. A light wreath starred with flowers rested on her hair. Gathering her draperies about her, she glanced disdainfully up and down the street while a footman, stooping, let down the step of the barouche landau. All Welbeck Street—for Welbeck Street it was—was wrapped in a splendour of red light—a light not clear and fierce like the Italian light, but tawny and troubled with the dust of a million wheels, with the trampling of a million hooves. The London season was at its height. A pall of sound, a cloud of interwoven humming, fell over the city in one confluent growl. By came a majestic deerhound led on a chain by a page. A policeman, swinging past with rhythmical stride, cast his bull's-eye from side to side. Odours of stew, odours of beef, odours of basting, odours of beef and cabbage rose from a thousand basements. A flunkey in livery dropped a letter into a box.

Overcome by the magnificence of the metropolis, Flush paused for a moment with his foot on the door-step. Wilson paused too. How paltry it seemed now, the civilization of Italy, its Courts and its revolutions, its Grand Dukes and their bodyguards! She thanked God, as the policeman passed, that she had not married Signor Righi after all. And then a sinister figure issued from the public-house at the corner. A man leered. With one spring Flush bolted indoors.

For some weeks now he was closely confined to a lodging-house sitting-room in Welbeck Street.* For confinement was still necessary. The cholera* had come, and it is true that the cholera had done something to improve the condition of the Rookeries; but not enough, for still dogs were stolen and the dogs of Wimpole Street had still to be led on chains. Flush went into society, of course. He met dogs at the pillar-box and outside the public-house; they welcomed him back with the inherent good breeding of their kind. Just as an English peer who has lived a lifetime in the East and contracted some of the habits of the natives—rumour hints indeed that he has turned Moslem and had a son by a Chinese washerwoman —finds, when he takes his place at Court, that old friends are ready enough to overlook these aberrations and he is asked to Chatsworth, though no mention is made of his wife and it is taken for granted that he will join the family at prayers—so the pointers and setters of Wimpole Street welcomed Flush among them and overlooked the condition of his coat. But there was a certain morbidity, it seemed to Flush now, among the dogs of London. It was common knowledge that Mrs Carlyle's dog Nero* had leapt from a top storey window[8] with the intention of committing suicide. He had found the strain of life in Cheyne Row intolerable, it was said. Indeed Flush could well believe it now that he was back again in Welbeck Street. The confinement, the crowd of little objects, the blackbeetles by night, the bluebottles by day, the lingering odours of mutton, the perpetual presence on the sideboard of bananas—all this, together with the proximity of several men and women, heavily dressed and not often or indeed completely washed, wrought on his temper and strained his nerves. He lay for hours under the lodging-house chiffonier. It was impossible to run out of doors. The front door was always locked. He had to wait for somebody to lead him on a chain.

Two incidents alone broke the monotony of the weeks he spent in London. One day late that summer the Brownings went to visit the Rev Charles Kingsley at Farnham.* In Italy the earth would have been bare and hard as brick. Fleas would have been rampant. Languidly one would have dragged oneself from shadow to shadow, grateful even for the bar of shade cast by the raised arm of one of Donatello's* statues. But here at Farnham there were fields of green grass; there were pools of blue water; there were woods that murmured; and turf so fine that the paws bounced as they touched it. The Brownings and the Kingsleys spent the day together. And once more, as Flush trotted behind them, the old trumpets blew; the old ecstasy returned—was it hare or was it fox? Flush tore over the heaths of Surrey as he had not run since the old days at Three Mile Cross. A pheasant went rocketing up in a spurt of purple and gold. He had almost shut his teeth on the tail feathers when a voice rang out. A whip cracked. Was it the Rev Charles Kingsley who called him sharply to heel? At any rate he ran no more. The woods of Farnham were strictly preserved.

A few days later he was lying in the sitting-room at Welbeck Street, when Mrs Browning came in dressed for walking and called him from under the chiffonier. She slipped the chain on to his collar and, for the first time since September 1846, they walked up Wimpole Street together. When they came to the door of No. 50 they stopped as of old. Just as of old they waited. The butler just as of old was very slow in coming. At length the door opened. Could that be Catiline lying couched on the mat? The old toothless dog yawned and stretched himself and took no notice. Upstairs they crept as stealthily, as silently as once before they had come down. Very quietly, opening the doors as if she were afraid of what she might see there, Mrs Browning went from room to room. A gloom descended upon her as she looked. '. . . they seemed to me', she wrote, 'smaller and darker, somehow, and the furniture wanted fitness and convenience.'* The ivy was still tapping on the back bedroom window-pane. The painted blind still obscured the houses. Nothing had been changed. Nothing had happened all these years. So she went from room to room, sadly remembering. But long before she had finished her inspection, Flush was in a fever of anxiety. Suppose Mr Barrett were to come in and find them? Suppose that with one frown he turned the key and locked them in the back bedroom for ever? At last Mrs Browning shut the doors and went downstairs again very quietly. Yes, she said, it seemed to her that the house wanted cleaning.

After that, Flush had only one wish left in him—to leave London, to leave England for ever. He was not happy until he found himself on the deck of the Channel steamer crossing to France. It was a rough passage. The crossing took eight hours. As the steamer tossed and wallowed, Flush turned over in his mind a tumult of mixed memories—of ladies in purple plush, of ragged men with bags; of Regent's Park, and Queen Victoria sweeping past with outriders; of the greenness of English grass and the rankness of English pavements—all this passed through his mind as he lay on deck; and, looking up, he caught sight of a stern, tall man leaning over the rail.

'Mr Carlyle!'* he heard Mrs Browning exclaim; where-upon—the crossing, it must be remembered, was a bad one—Flush was violently sick. Sailors came running with pails and mops. '. . . he was ordered off the deck on purpose, poor dog',* said Mrs Browning. For the deck was still English; dogs must not be sick on decks. Such was his last salute to the shores of his native land.

CHAPTER VI

THE END

FLUSH was growing an old dog now. The journey to England and all the memories it revived had undoubtedly tired him. It was noticed that he sought the shade rather than the sun on his return, though the shade of Florence was hotter than the sun of Wimpole Street. Stretched beneath a statue, couched under the lip of a fountain for the sake of the few drops that spurted now and again on to his coat, he would lie dozing by the hour. The young dogs would come about him. To them he would tell his stories of Whitechapel and Wimpole Street; he would describe the smell of clover and the smell of Oxford Street; he would rehearse his memories of one revolution and another—how Grand Dukes had come and Grand Dukes had gone; but the spotted spaniel down the alley on the left—she goes on for ever, he would say. Then violent Mr Landor would hurry by and shake his fist at him in mock fury; kind Miss Isa Blagden would pause and take a sugared biscuit from her reticule. The peasant women in the market-place made him a bed of leaves in the shadow of their baskets and tossed him a bunch of grapes now and then. He was known, he was liked by all Florence—gentle and simple, dogs and men.

But he was growing an old dog now, and he tended more and more to lie not even under the fountain—for the cobbles were too hard for his old bones—but in Mrs Browning's bedroom where the arms of the Guidi family made a smooth patch of scagliola on the floor, or in the drawing-room under the shadow of the drawing-room table. One day shortly after his return from London he was stretched there fast asleep. The deep and dreamless sleep of old age was heavy on him. Indeed to-day his sleep was deeper even than usual, for as he slept the darkness seemed to thicken round him. If he dreamt at all, he dreamt that he was sleeping in the heart of a primeval forest, shut from the light of the sun, shut from the voices of mankind, though now and again as he slept he dreamt that he heard the sleepy chirp of a dreaming bird, or, as the wind tossed the branches, the mellow chuckle of a brooding monkey.

Then suddenly the branches parted; the light broke in—here, there, in dazzling shafts. Monkeys chattered; birds rose crying and calling in alarm. He started to his feet wide awake. An astonishing commotion was all round him. He had fallen asleep between the bare legs of an ordinary drawing-room table. Now he was hemmed in by the billowing of skirts and the heaving of trousers. The table itself, moreover, was swaying violently from side to side. He did not know which way to run. What on earth was happening? What in Heaven's name possessed the drawing-room table? He lifted up his voice in a prolonged howl of interrogation.

To Flush's question no satisfactory answer can here be given. A few facts, and those of the baldest, are all that can be supplied. Briefly, then, it would appear that early in the nineteenth century the Countess of Blessington* had bought a crystal ball from a magician. Her Ladyship 'never could understand the use of it'; indeed she had never been able to see anything in the ball except crystal. After her death, however, there was a sale of her effects and the ball came into the possession of others who 'looked deeper, or with purer eyes' and saw other things in the ball besides crystal. Whether Lord Stanhope* was the purchaser, whether it was he who looked 'with purer eyes', is not stated. But certainly by the year 1852 Lord Stanhope was in possession of a crystal ball and Lord Stanhope had only to look into it to see among other things 'the spirits of the sun'. Obviously this was not a sight that a hospitable nobleman could keep to himself, and Lord Stanhope was in the habit of displaying his ball at luncheon parties and of inviting his friends to see the spirits of the sun also. There was something strangely delightful—except indeed to Mr Chorley*—in the spectacle; balls became the rage; and luckily a London optician soon discovered that he could make them, without being either an Egyptian or a magician, though naturally the price of English crystal was high. Thus many people in the early 'fifties became possessed of balls, though 'many persons', Lord Stanhope said, 'use the balls, without the moral courage to confess it'. The prevalence of spirits in London indeed became so marked that some alarm was felt; and Lord Stanley suggested to Sir Edward Lytton 'that the Government should appoint a committee of investigation so as to get as far as possible at the facts'.* Whether the rumour of an approaching Government committee alarmed the spirits, or whether spirits, like bodies, tend to multiply in close confinement, there can be no doubt that the spirits began to show signs of restlessness, and, escaping in vast numbers, took up their residence in the legs of tables. Whatever the motive, the policy was successful. Crystal balls were expensive; almost everybody owns a table. Thus when Mrs Browning returned to Italy in the winter of 1852 she found that the spirits had preceded her; the tables of Florence were almost universally infected. 'From the Legation to the

English chemists', she wrote, 'people are "serving tables" . . . everywhere. When people gather round a table it isn't to play whist.'* No, it was to decipher messages conveyed by the legs of tables. Thus if asked the age of a child, the table 'expresses itself intelligently by knocking with its legs, responses according to the alphabet'.* And if a table could tell you that your own child was four years old, what limit was there to its capacity? Spinning tables were advertised in shops. The walls were placarded with advertisements of wonders 'scoperte a Livorno'.* By the year 1854, so rapidly did the movement spread, 'four hundred thousand families in America had given their names . . . as actually in enjoyment of spiritual intercourse'.* And from England the news came that Sir Edward Bulwer Lytton had imported 'several of the American rapping spirits' to Knebworth, with the happy result—so little Arthur Russell* was informed when he beheld a 'strange-looking old gentleman in a shabby dressing-gown' staring at him at breakfast—that Sir Edward Bulwer Lytton believed himself invisible.[9]

When Mrs Browning first looked into Lord Stanhope's crystal ball at a luncheon party she saw nothing—except indeed that it was a remarkable sign of the times. The spirit of the sun indeed told her that she was about to go to Rome; but as she was not about to go to Rome, she contradicted the spirits of the sun. 'But', she added, with truth, 'I love the marvellous'.* She was nothing if not adventurous. She had gone to Manning Street at the risk of her life. She had discovered a world that she had never dreamt of within half an hour's drive from Wimpole Street. Why should there not be another world only half a moment's flight from Florence—a better world, a more beautiful world, where the dead live, trying in vain to reach us? At any rate she would take the risk. And so she sat herself down at the table too. And Mr Lytton, the brilliant son of an invisible father, came; and Mr Frederick Tennyson, and Mr Powers and M. Villari*—they all sat at the table, and then when the table had done kicking, they sat on drinking tea and eating strawberries and cream, with 'Florence dissolving in the purple of the hills and the stars looking on', talking and talking: '. . . what stories we told, and what miracles we swore to! Oh, we are believers here, Isa, except Robert . . .'* Then in burst deaf Mr Kirkup* with his bleak white beard. He had come round simply to exclaim, 'There is a spiritual world—there is a future state. I confess it. I am convinced at last.' And when Mr Kirkup, whose creed had always been 'the next thing to atheism', was converted merely because, in spite of his deafness, he had heard 'three taps so loud that they made him leap', how could Mrs Browning keep her hands off the table? 'You know I am rather a visionary and inclined to knock round at all the doors of the present world to try to get out',* she wrote. So she summoned the faithful to Casa Guidi; and there they sat with their hands on the drawing-room table, trying to get out.

Flush started up in the wildest apprehension. The skirts and the trousers were billowing round him; the table was standing on one leg. But whatever the ladies and gentlemen round the table could hear and see, Flush could hear and see nothing. True, the table was standing on one leg, but so tables will if you lean hard on one side. He had upset tables himself and been well scolded for it. But now there was Mrs Browning with her great eyes wide open staring as if she saw something marvellous outside. Flush rushed to the balcony and looked over. Was there another Grand Duke riding by with banners and torches? Flush could see nothing but an old beggar woman crouched at the corner of the street over her basket of melons. Yet clearly Mrs Browning saw something; clearly she saw something that was very wonderful. So in the old Wimpole Street days she had wept once without any reason that he could see; and again she had laughed, holding up a blotted scrawl. But this was different. There was something in her look now that frightened him. There was something in the room, or in the table, or in the petticoats and trousers, that he disliked exceedingly.

As the weeks passed, this preoccupation of Mrs Browning's with the invisible grew upon her. It might be a fine hot day, but instead of watching the lizards slide in and out of the stones, she would sit at the table; it might be a dark starry night, but instead of reading in her book, or passing her hand over paper, she would call, if Mr Browning were out, for Wilson, and Wilson would come yawning. Then they would sit at the table together until that article of furniture, whose chief function it was to provide shade, kicked on the floor, and Mrs Browning exclaimed that it was telling Wilson that she would soon be ill. Wilson replied that she was only sleepy. But soon Wilson herself, the implacable, the upright, the British, screamed and went into a faint, and Mrs Browning was rushing hither and thither to find 'the hygienic vinegar'. That, to Flush, was a highly unpleasant way of spending a quiet evening. Better far to sit and read one's book.

Undoubtedly the suspense, the intangible but disagreeable odour, the kicks and the screams and the vinegar, told upon Flush's nerves. It was all very well for the baby, Penini, to pray 'that Flush's hair may grow';* that was an aspiration that Flush could understand. But this form of prayer which required the presence of evil-smelling, seedy-looking men and the antics of a piece of apparently solid mahogany, angered him much as they angered that robust, sensible, well-dressed man, his master. But far worse than any smell to Flush, far worse than any antics, was the look of Mrs Browning's face when she gazed out of the window as if she were seeing something that was wonderful when there was nothing. Flush stood himself in front of her. She looked through him as if he were not there. That was the cruellest look she had ever given him. It was worse than her cold anger when he bit Mr Browning in the leg; worse than her sardonic laughter when the door shut upon his paw in Regent's Park. There were moments indeed when he regretted Wimpole Street and its tables. The tables at No. 50 had never tilted upon one leg. The little table with the ring round it that held her precious ornaments had always stood perfectly still. In those far-off days he had only to leap on her sofa and Miss Barrett started wide-awake and looked at him. Now, once more, he leapt on to her sofa. But she did not notice him. She was writing. She paid no attention to him. She went on writing—'also, at the request of the medium, the spiritual hands took from the table a garland which lay there, and placed it upon my head. The particular hand which did this was of the largest human size, as white as snow, and very beautiful. It was as near to me as this hand I write with, and I saw it as distinctly.'* Flush pawed her sharply. She looked through him as if he were invisible. He leapt off the sofa and ran downstairs into the street.

It was a blazing hot afternoon. The old beggar woman at the corner had fallen asleep over her melons. The sun seemed droning in the sky. Keeping to the shady side of the street,

Flush trotted along the well-known ways to the market-place. The whole square was brilliant with awnings and stalls and bright umbrellas. The market women were sitting beside baskets of fruit; pigeons were fluttering, bells were pealing, whips were cracking. The many-coloured mongrels of Florence were running in and out sniffing and pawing. All was as brisk as a bee-hive and as hot as an oven. Flush sought the shade. He flung himself down beside his friend Catterina, under the shadow of her great basket. A brown jar of red and yellow flowers cast a shadow beside it. Above them a statue, holding his right arm outstretched, deepened the shade to violet. Flush lay there in the cool, watching the young dogs busy with their own affairs. They were snarling and biting, stretching and tumbling, in all the abandonment of youthful joy. They were chasing each other in and out, round and round, as he had once chased the spotted spaniel in the alley. His thoughts turned to Reading for a moment—to Mr Partridge's spaniel, to his first love, to the ecstasies, the innocence of youth. Well, he had had his day. He did not grudge them theirs. He had found the world a pleasant place to live in. He had no quarrel with it now. The market woman scratched him behind the ear. She had often cuffed him for stealing a grape, or for some other misdemeanour; but he was old now; and she was old. He guarded her melons and she scratched his ear. So she knitted and he dozed. The flies buzzed on the great pink melon that had been sliced open to show its flesh.

The sun burnt deliciously through the lily leaves, and through the green and white umbrella. The marble statue tempered its heat to a champagne freshness. Flush lay and let it burn through his fur to the naked skin. And when he was roasted on one side he turned over and let the sun roast the other. All the time the market people were chattering and bargaining; market women were passing; they were stopping and fingering the vegetables and the fruit. There was a perpetual buzz and hum of human voices such as Flush loved to listen to. After a time he drowsed off under the shadow of the lilies. He slept as dogs sleep when they are dreaming. Now his legs twitched—was he dreaming that he hunted rabbits in Spain? Was he coursing up a hot hill-side with dark men shouting 'Span! Span!' as the rabbits darted from the brushwood? Then he lay still again. And now he yelped, quickly, softly, many times in succession. Perhaps he heard Dr Mitford egging his greyhounds on to the hunt at Reading. Then his tail wagged sheepishly. Did he hear old Miss Mitford cry 'Bad dog! Bad dog!' as he slunk back to her, where she stood among the turnips waving her umbrella? And then he lay for a time snoring, wrapt in the deep sleep of happy old age. Suddenly every muscle in his body twitched. He woke with a violent start. Where did he think he was? In White-chapel among the ruffians? Was the knife at his throat again?

Whatever it was, he woke from his dream in a state of terror. He made off as if he were flying to safety, as if he were seeking refuge. The market women laughed and pelted him with rotten grapes and called him back. He took no notice. Cartwheels almost crushed him as he darted through the streets—the men standing up to drive cursed him and flicked him with their whips. Half-naked children threw pebbles at him and shouted '*Matta! Matta!*'* as he fled past. Their mothers ran to the door and caught them back in alarm. Had he then gone mad? Had the sun turned his brain? Or had he once more heard the hunting horn of Venus? Or had one of the American rapping spirits, one of the spirits that live in table legs, got possession of him at last? Whatever it was, he went in a bee-line up one street and down another until he reached the door of Casa Guidi. He made his way straight upstairs and went straight into the drawing-room.

Mrs Browning was lying, reading, on the sofa. She looked up, startled, as he came in. No, it was not a spirit—it was only Flush. She laughed. Then, as he leapt on to the sofa and thrust his face into hers, the words of her own poem came into her mind:

> You see this dog. It was but yesterday
> I mused forgetful of his presence here
> Till thought on thought drew downward tear on tear,
> When from the pillow, where wet-cheeked I lay,
> A head as hairy as Faunus, thrust its way
> Right sudden against my face,—two golden-clear
> Great eyes astonished mine,—a drooping ear
> Did flap me on either cheek to dry the spray!
> I started first, as some Arcadian,
> Amazed by goatly god in twilight grove;
> But, as the bearded vision closelier ran
> My tears off, I knew Flush, and rose above
> Surprise and sadness,—thanking the true Pan,
> Who, by low creatures, leads to heights of love.

She had written that poem one day years ago in Wimpole Street when she was very unhappy. Now she was happy. She was growing old now and so was Flush. She bent down over him for a moment. Her face with its wide mouth and its great eyes and its heavy curls was still oddly like his. Broken asunder, yet made in the same mould, each, perhaps, completed what was dormant in the other. But she was woman; he was dog. Mrs Browning went on reading. Then she looked at Flush again. But he did not look at her. An extraordinary change had come over him. 'Flush!' she cried. But he was silent. He had been alive; he was now dead.[10] That was all. The drawing-room table, strangely enough, stood perfectly still.*

AUTHORITIES

It must be admitted that there are very few authorities for the foregoing biography. But the reader who would like to check the facts or to pursue the subject further is referred to:

To Flush, My Dog.
Flush, or Faunus. } Poems by Elizabeth Barrett Browning

The Letters of Robert Browning and Elizabeth Barrett Browning. 2 vols.

The Letters of Elizabeth Barrett Browning, edited by Frederick Kenyon. 2 vols.

The Letters of Elizabeth Barrett Browning addressed to Richard Hengist Horne, edited by S. R. Townshend Mayer. 2 vols.

Elizabeth Barrett Browning: Letters to her sister 1846–1859, edited by Leonard Huxley, LL.D.

Elizabeth Barrett Browning in her Letters, by Percy Lubbock.

References to Flush are to be found in the *Letters of Mary Russell Mitford*, edited by H. Chorley, 2 vols.

For an account of London Rookeries, *The Rookeries of London*, by Thomas Beames, 1850, may be consulted.

WOOLF'S NOTES

1. 'painted fabric'. Miss Barrett says, 'I had a transparent blind put up in my open window'. She adds, 'papa insults me with the analogy of a back window in a confectioner's shop, but is obviously moved when the sunshine lights up the castle, notwithstanding'. Some hold that the castle, etc., was painted on a thin metallic substance; others that it was a muslin blind richly embroidered. There seems no certain way of settling the matter.

2. 'Mr Kenyon mumbled slightly because he had lost two front teeth.' There are elements of exaggeration and conjecture here. Miss Mitford is the authority. She is reported to have said in conversation with Mr Horne, 'Our dear friend, you are aware, never sees anybody but the members of her own family, and one or two others. She has a high opinion of the skill in *reading* as well as the fine taste, of Mr ——, and she gets him to read her new poems aloud to her. . . . So Mr —— stands upon the hearth-rug, and uplifts the MS, and his voice, while our dear friend lies folded up in Indian shawls upon her sofa, with her long black tresses streaming over her bent-down head, all attention. Now, dear Mr —— has lost a front tooth—not quite a front one, but a side front one—and this, you see, causes a defective utterance . . . an amiable indistinctness, a vague softening of syllables into each other, so that silence and ilence would really sound very like one another . . .' There can be little doubt that Mr —— was Mr Kenyon; the blank was necessitated by the peculiar delicacy of the Victorians with regard to teeth. But more important questions affecting English literature are involved. Miss Barrett has long been accused of a defective ear. Miss Mitford maintains that Mr Kenyon

should rather be accused of defective teeth. On the other hand, Miss Barrett herself maintained that her rhymes had nothing to do with his lack of teeth or with her lack of ear. 'A great deal of attention', she wrote, '—far more than it would have taken to rhyme with complete accuracy—have I given to the subject of rhymes and have determined in cold blood to hazard some experiments.' Hence she rhymed 'angels' with 'candles', 'heaven' with 'unbelieving', and 'islands' with 'silence'—in cold blood. It is of course for the professors to decide; but anybody who has studied Mrs Browning's character and her actions will be inclined to take the view that she was a wilful breaker of rules whether of art or of love, and so to convict her of some complicity in the development of modern poetry.

3. 'yellow gloves'. It is recorded in Mrs Orr's Life of Browning that he wore lemon-coloured gloves. Mrs Bridell-Fox, meeting him in 1835–6, says, 'he was then slim and dark, and very handsome, and—may I hint it—just a trifle of a dandy, addicted to lemon-coloured kid gloves and such things'.

4. 'He was stolen.' As a matter of fact, Flush was stolen three times; but the unities seem to require that the three stealings shall be compressed into one. The total sum paid by Miss Barrett to the dog-stealers was £20.

5. 'The faces of those men were to come back to her on a sunny balcony in Italy.' Readers of Aurora Leigh—but since such persons are non-existent it must be explained that Mrs Browning wrote a poem of this name, one of the most vivid passages in which (though it suffers from distortion natural to an artist who sees the object once only from a four-wheeler, with Wilson tugging at her skirts) is the description of a London slum. Clearly Mrs Browning possessed a fund of curiosity as to human life which was by no means satisfied by the busts of Homer and Chaucer on the washing-stand in the bedroom.

6. 'Lily Wilson fell in love with Signor Righi, the guardsman.' The life of Lily Wilson is extremely obscure and thus cries aloud for the services of a biographer. No human figure in the Browning

letters, save the principals, more excites our curiosity and
baffles it. Her Christian name was Lily, her surname Wilson.
That is all we know of her birth and upbringing. Whether she
was the daughter of a farmer in the neighbourhood of Hope
End, and became favourably known to the Barrett cook by the
decency of her demeanour and the cleanliness of her apron, so
much so that when she came up to the great house on some
errand, Mrs Barrett made an excuse to come into the room just
then and thought so well of her that she appointed her to be
Miss Elizabeth's maid; or whether she was a Cockney; or
whether she was from Scotland—it is impossible to say. At any
rate she was in service with Miss Barrett in the year 1846. She
was 'an expensive servant'—her wages were £16 a year. Since
she spoke almost as seldom as Flush, the outlines of her
character are little known; and since Miss Barrett never wrote a
poem about her, her appearance is far less familiar than his. Yet
it is clear from indications in the letters that she was in the
beginning one of those demure, almost inhumanly correct
British maids who were at that time the glory of the British
basement. It is obvious that Wilson was a stickler for rights and
ceremonies. Wilson undoubtedly revered 'the room'; Wilson
would have been the first to insist that under servants must eat
their pudding in one place, upper servants in another. All this is
implicit in the remark she made when she beat Flush with her
hand 'because it is right'. Such respect for convention, it need
hardly be said, breeds extreme horror of any breach of it; so that
when Wilson was confronted with the lower orders in Manning
Street she was far more alarmed, and far more certain that the
dog-stealers were murderers, than Miss Barrett was. At the
same time the heroic way in which she overcame her terror and
went with Miss Barrett in the cab shows how deeply the other
convention of loyalty to her mistress was ingrained in her.
Where Miss Barrett went, Wilson must go too. This principle
was triumphantly demonstrated by her conduct at the time of
the elopement. Miss Barrett had been doubtful of Wilson's
courage; but her doubts were unfounded. 'Wilson', she wrote

—and these were the last words she ever wrote to Mr Browning as Miss Barrett—'has been perfect to me. And *I* . . . calling her "timid" and afraid of her timidity! I begin to think that none are so bold as the timid, when they are fairly roused.' It is worth, parenthetically, dwelling for a second on the extreme precariousness of a servant's life. If Wilson had not gone with Miss Barrett, she would have been, as Miss Barrett knew, 'turned into the street before sunset', with only a few shillings, presumably, saved from her sixteen pounds a year. And what then would have been her fate? Since English fiction in the 'forties scarcely deals with the lives of ladies' maids, and biography had not then cast its searchlight so low, the question must remain a question. But Wilson took the plunge. She declared that she would 'go anywhere in the world with me'. She left the basement, the room, the whole of that world of Wimpole Street, which to Wilson meant all civilization, all right thinking and decent living, for the wild debauchery and irreligion of a foreign land. Nothing is more curious than to observe the conflict that took place in Italy between Wilson's English gentility and her natural passions. She derided the Italian Court; she was shocked by Italian pictures. But, though 'she was struck back by the indecency of the Venus', Wilson, greatly to her credit, seems to have bethought her that women are naked when they take their clothes off. Even I myself, she may have thought, am naked for two or three seconds daily. And so 'She thinks she shall try again, and the troublesome modesty may subside, who knows?' That it did subside rapidly is plain. Soon she not merely approved of Italy; she had fallen in love with Signor Righi of the Grand Ducal bodyguard— 'all highly respectable and moral men, and some six feet high'—was wearing an engagement ring; was dismissing a London suitor; and was learning to speak Italian. Then the clouds descend again; when they lift they show us Wilson deserted—'the faithless Righi had backed out of his engagement to Wilson'. Suspicion attaches to his brother, a wholesale haberdasher at Prato. When Righi resigned from the

Ducal bodyguard, he became, on his brother's advice, a retail haberdasher at Prato. Whether his position required a know-ledge of haberdashery in his wife, whether one of the girls of Prato could supply it, it is certain that he did not write to Wilson as often as he should have done. But what conduct it was on the part of this highly respectable and moral man that led Mrs Browning to exclaim in 1850, '[Wilson] is *over* it completely, which does the greatest credit to her good sense and rectitude of character. How could she continue to love such a man?'—why Righi had shrunk to 'such a man' in so short a time, it is impossible to say. Deserted by Righi, Wilson became more and more attached to the Browning family. She discharged not only the duties of a lady's maid, but cooked knead cakes, made dresses, and became a devoted nurse to Penini, the baby; so that in time the baby himself exalted her to the rank of the family, where she justly belonged, and refused to call her anything but Lily. In 1855 Wilson married Romagnoli, the Brownings' manservant, 'a good tender-hearted man'; and for some time the two kept house for the Brownings. But in 1859 Robert Browning 'accepted office of Landor's guardian', an office of great delicacy and responsibility, for Landor's habits were difficult; 'of restraint he has not a grain', Mrs Browning wrote, 'and of suspiciousness many grains'. In these cir-cumstances Wilson was appointed 'his duenna' with a salary of twenty-two pounds a year 'besides what is left of his rations'. Later her wages were increased to thirty pounds, for to act as duenna to 'an old lion' who has 'the impulses of a tiger', throws his plate out of the window or dashes it on the ground if he dislikes his dinner, and suspects servants of opening desks, entailed, as Mrs Browning observed, 'certain risks, and I for one would rather not meet them'. But to Wilson, who had known Mr Barrett and the spirits, a few plates more or less flying out of the window or dashed upon the floor was a matter of little consequence—such risks were all in the day's work.

That day, so far as it is still visible to us, was certainly a strange one. Whether it began or not in some remote English

village, it ended in Venice in the Palazzo Rezzonico. There at
least she was still living in the year 1897, a widow, in the house
of the little boy whom she had nursed and loved—Mr Barrett
Browning. A very strange day it had been, she may have
thought, as she sat in the red Venetian sunset, an old woman,
dreaming. Her friends, married to farm hands, still stumbled
up the English lanes to fetch a pint of beer. And she had eloped
with Miss Barrett to Italy; she had seen all kinds of queer
things—revolutions, guardsmen, spirits; Mr Landor throwing
his plate out of the window. Then Mrs Browning had died
—there can have been no lack of thoughts in Wilson's old head
as she sat at the window of the Palazzo Rezzonico in the
evening. But nothing can be more vain than to pretend that we
can guess what they were, for she was typical of the great army
of her kind—the inscrutable, the all-but-silent, the all-but-
invisible servant maids of history. 'A more honest, true and
affectionate heart than Wilson's cannot be found'—her mistress's words may serve her for epitaph.

7. 'he was scourged by fleas'. It appears that Italy was famous for
its fleas in the middle of the nineteenth century. Indeed, they
served to break down conventions that were otherwise in-
surmountable. For example, when Nathaniel Hawthorne went
to tea with Miss Bremer in Rome (1858), 'we spoke of fleas
—insects that, in Rome, come home to everybody's business
and bosom, and are so common and inevitable, that no delicacy
is felt about alluding to the sufferings they inflict. Poor little
Miss Bremer was tormented with one while turning out our
tea. . . .'

8. 'Nero had leapt from a top storey window.' Nero (*c.* 1849–60)
was, according to Carlyle, 'A little Cuban (Maltese? and
otherwise mongrel) shock, mostly white—a most affectionate,
lively little dog, otherwise of small merit, and little or no
training'. Material for a life of him abounds, but this is not the
occasion to make use of it. It is enough to say that he was stolen;
that he brought Carlyle a cheque to buy a horse with tied round

his neck; that 'twice or thrice I flung him into the sea [at Aberdour], which he didn't at all like'; that in 1850 he sprang from the library window, and, clearing the area spikes, fell 'plash' on to the pavement. 'It was after breakfast,' Mrs Carlyle says, 'and he had been standing at the open window, watching the birds . . . Lying in my bed, I heard thro' the deal partition Elizabeth scream: Oh God! oh Nero! and rush downstairs like a strong wind out at the street door . . . then I sprang to meet her in my night-shift . . . Mr C came down from his bedroom with his chin all over soap and asked, "Has anything happened to Nero?"—"Oh, sir, he *must* have broken all his legs, he leapt out at *your* window!"—"God bless me!" said Mr C and returned to finish his shaving.' No bones were broken, however, and he survived; to be run over by a butcher's cart, and to die at last from the effects of the accident on 1st February 1860. He is buried at the top of the garden at Cheyne Row under a small stone tablet.

Whether he wished to kill himself, or whether, as Mrs Carlyle insinuates, he was merely jumping after birds, might be the occasion for an extremely interesting treatise on canine psychology. Some hold that Byron's dog went mad in sympathy with Byron; others that Nero was driven to desperate melancholy by associating with Mr Carlyle. The whole question of dogs' relation to the spirit of the age, whether it is possible to call one dog Elizabethan, another Augustan, another Victorian, together with the influence upon dogs of the poetry and philosophy of their masters, deserves a fuller discussion than can here be given it. For the present, Nero's motives must remain obscure.

9. 'Sir Edward Bulwer Lytton believed himself invisible.' Mrs Huth Jackson in *A Victorian Childhood* says: 'Lord Arthur Russell told me, many years later, that when a small boy he was taken to Knebworth by his mother. Next morning he was in the big hall having breakfast when a strange-looking old gentleman in a shabby dressing-gown came in and walked slowly round

the table staring at each of the guests in turn. He heard his mother's neighbour whisper to her, "Do not take any notice, he thinks he is invisible." It was Lord Lytton himself' (pp. 17–18).

10. 'he was now dead'. It is certain that Flush died; but the date and manner of his death are unknown. The only reference consists in the statement that 'Flush lived to a good old age and is buried in the vaults of Casa Guidi'. Mrs Browning was buried in the English Cemetery at Florence, Robert Browning in Westminster Abbey. Flush still lies, therefore, beneath the house in which, once upon a time, the Brownings lived.

EDITOR'S NOTES

Beames   Thomas Beames, *The Rookeries of London: Past, Present, and Prospective* (London: Thomas Bosworth, 1850).

Dalziel   Dalziel, *British Dogs: Their Varieties, History and Characteristics* (London: L. Upcott Gill [1887]), vol. 1.

EBRB   *The Letters of Robert Browning and Elizabeth Barrett Barrett 1845–1846*, 2 vols. (London: Smith, Elder, & Co., 1899).

EBB/RH   *Letters of Elizabeth Barrett Browning addressed to Richard Hengist Horne*, ed. S. R. Townshend Mayer (2 vols., London: Richard Bentley, 1877).

EBBL   *The Letters of Elizabeth Barrett Browning.* Edited with biographical additions by Frederic G. Kenyon. (2 vols., London: Smith, Elder, 1897).

EBBS   *Elizabeth Barrett Browning: Letters to her sister, 1846–1859* ed. Leonard Huxley (London: John Murray, 1929).

MLife   *The Life of Mary Russell Mitford related in a selection from her letters to her friends* ed. Revd A. G. L'Estrange (3 vols., London: Richard Bentley, 1870).

MRM   *Letters of Mary Russell Mitford*, 2nd ser., 2 vols. (London: Richard Bentley & Son, 1872).

OED   *Oxford English Dictionary*

5 *one of the greatest antiquity*: Woolf took her information about spaniels from Dalziel, pp. 380 ff.

Hispania, or Rabbit-land: Dalziel, p. 386.

6 *Howel Dha*: Dalziel, p. 383. Howel Dha, d. 950, was called in

the prologues to Welsh law books the 'king of all Wales', and for the last years of his life more nearly held that position than any previous ruler.

Howards ... Cavendishes ... Russells: Howard is the ancient family name of the Duke of Norfolk, first duke of the realm and hereditary earl marshal of England; Cavendish the family name of the Duke of Devonshire; Russell the name of a prominent Whig family, the senior line of which has held the title of Duke of Bedford since the late seventeenth century.

7 *Clumber ... Sussex ... Norfolk ... Black Field ... Cocker ... Irish Water ... English Water*: Dalziel, p. 380.

'*... greyhounds ... Yeomen of dogs*': Sir Philip Sidney, *The Countess of Pembroke's Arcadia: (the new Arcadia)* (1590) ed. Victor Skretkowitcz (Oxford: Clarendon Press, 1987), 142. Woolf was writing her article 'The Countess of Pembroke's Arcadia' in 1931–2 (finishing it on 26 February 1932); it was published in *The Common Reader* (second series), 1932.

the Spaniel Club: formed 1886 (Dalziel, p. 389).

gozzled: not in the *OED*, but by inference (gozell = gooseberry or currant), prominent.

8 *Heralds' College*: or College of Arms: a royal corporation, founded 1483, consisting of the earl marshal, kings-of-arms, heralds, and pursuivants; initially exercising jurisdiction in armorial matters, and coming to record proved pedigrees and to grant armorial bearings.

Bourbon, Hapsburg and Hohenzollern: the Bourbon was one of the most important ruling houses of Europe, its members descending from Louis I, duc de Bourbon 1327–42. They ruled in France (1589–1792; 1814–48), Spain (1700–1931), Naples and Sicily (*c*.1734–1860). The Hapsburg (also known as the House of Austria) was one of the principal sovereign dynasties of Europe from the fifteenth to the twentieth centuries, ruling Spain until 1700, and holding possessions in Central Europe until 1918. The Hohenzollern were chiefly prominent as the rulers of Brandenburg–Prussia (1415–1918) and imperial Germany (1871–1918).

8 *Dr . . . Mitford*: George Mitford trained as a doctor but never worked. He was an excellent whist-player but an unlucky gambler, which meant that the family were continually very short of money.

Miss Russell: Mary Russell, an heiress.

9 *his daughter's*: Mary Russell Mitford (1787–1855), only daughter of Mary and George Mitford. She is best known for her collection of essays, *Our Village, sketches of rural life, character, and scenery*, begun in the *Lady's Magazine* (1819) and published separately 1824–32. These are set in Three Mile Cross, near Reading, where she lived with her parents.

Apollo: also called Phoebus, identified with the sun: son of Zeus and Latona; god of music and poetry (and who founds states and colonies), and the type of manly beauty.

Bacchus: or Dionysius: god of fertility, and, particularly, of wine.

Flush's birth: Flush's father was also called Flush: he dies 1 December 1847 (see MM to Emily Jephson, 4 July 1838, *M Life* iii, 88–9; *MRM* i, 242).

the year 1842: Woolf is mistaken: EB writes to MM and Dr Mitford from Torquay in December 1840 thanking them for 'Flush the second': 'No dog in the world could please me so.' She tries to return him on 28 December since she has realized that he is a valuable dog (her awareness of his monetary value to the Mitfords is masked behind an anxiety that if he is taken away from sporting pursuits and kept as a pet he will be 'exposed to a martyrdom'). On 2 January 1841, as a result of their protestations, she agrees to keep him. See *Elizabeth Barrett to Miss Mitford: The Unpublished Letters of Elizabeth Barrett to Mary Russell Mitford*, ed. Betty Miller, (London: John Murray, 1954), 68–70. EB's letter of 21 September 1841 describes the enjoyment Flush took in his journey to London,

his arrival in Wimpole Street, and his continual in-
quisitiveness ('I am by no means sure that Flush wont bring
out as good a two volumes of "Travels" some day—of notes
and documents—as anybody from the new world': ibid. 86–7).
A letter of 18 August 1842 tells us that he 'hates the drawing
room. It is Blue Beards' lock up room to him' (ibid. 129); that of
7 January 1843 (ibid. 162–4) gives an extended description of
his liveliness and affection; that of 23 June 1843 (ibid. 184–5)
recounts Flush being taken to see the military review in Hyde
Park, and apparently frightened, running home on his own;
she also tells of his enjoyment of cayenne pepper and ginger
cake.

Tray: the 'poor dog' of Thomas Campbell's 'The Harper'
(1799): the name of one of the family dogs of RB's childhood,
and RB wrote an anti-vivisection poem 'Tray', published in
Dramatic Idyls (1879).

10 *'real old cocking spaniel . . . excellence in the field'*: MM to Mrs
Partridge, 3 July 1846, *MRM* i, 222.

to poetry, alas: Elizabeth Barrett Browning's poem 'To Flush,
My Dog' (1844).

Kerenhappock: MM, writing to EB, describes the maid as 'a
young woman of remarkable intelligence and presence of
mind' (*MLife* iii, 127). The Mitfords also, in fact, had a
manservant at this time, Ben Kirby.

cribbage: game played by two, three, or four persons, with a
complete pack of 52 cards, five or six of which are dealt to each
player, and a board with sixty-one holes on which the points
are scored by means of pegs.

12 *Venus*: Roman name for goddess of beauty and love.

Dr Pusey: Edward Bouverie Pusey (1800–82): Regius professor
of Hebrew at the University of Oxford, and a High Anglican
who was a member of the so-called Oxford Movement in the
1830s, and later tried to bring about the union of the English
and Roman Catholic Churches.

12 *'I have not bought ... for four years'*: MM to Emily Jephson, 10 January 1842 (*MLife* iii, 117).

13 *Elizabeth Barrett*: Elizabeth Barrett Browning (1806–61), poet.

14 *Corinth has fallen and Messina has tumbled*: Corinth was a commercial centre from the eighth century BC, under the Greeks, Romans, and Byzantines: it was reduced to a small town after the Turkish consquest of 1458. Messina, a strategically important Sicilian town from *c.*730 BC, was severely damaged by an earthquake in 1783 and almost totally destroyed by one in 1908.

15 *a house in Shropshire*: the estate of Hope End was in fact in the eastern part of Herefordshire. EB writing to Robert Browning (11 July 1845: *EDRB* i, 119) described the house that her father built as a 'Turkish house ... crowded with minarets and domes, and crowned with metal spires and crescents.' Edward Moulton Barrett's financial position meant that Hope End—then valued at about £50,000—was seized and put up for sale to satisfy his creditors in the spring of 1831.

his East Indian property: Woolf's geography is at fault: the property was in the West Indies. Edward Barrett's grandfather owned substantial property, and slaves, at Cinnamon Hill, Jamaica. These plantations experienced widespread destruction in the slave uprisings of 1831–2.

20 *houses made almost entirely of glass*: Woolf is premature in her dating of the growth of the department store with their plate-glass window displays: glass technology developed in this area after the 1851 Great Exhibition.

24 *Wilson, Miss Barrett's maid*: Elizabeth Wilson, engaged April 1844.

26 *'Flushie ... is my friend ... without'*: Elizabeth Barrett to Richard Horne, 5 October 1843: *EBB/RH* i, 165. EBB was writing to RH after Flush had been stolen for the first time: 'Oh, and if you had seen him, when he came home and threw himself into my arms, palpitating with joy—in that dumb

inarticulate ecstasy which is so affecting—love without speech!' See also EBB to H. S. Boyd, 19 September 1843, *EBBL* i, 155.

'*A bird . . . good a story*': *EBBL* i. 158.

Mr Kenyon: John Kenyon (1784–1857), son of another Jamaican family and a distant cousin; poet, and friend of poets, including Wordsworth, Southey, and Walter Landor, and patron of the arts.

27 '*Ah, my dear Mr Horne . . . the failure in my health . . . the enforced exile to Torquay . . . a nightmare to my life . . . Mr Horne*': Richard Henry (later Hengist) Horne (1803–84): editor, journalist, government officer, poet, dramatist, and critic. He corresponded with Elizabeth Barrett from 1839, when they first met. In the autumn of 1838, the invalid EB travelled to Torquay, so that she should not have to face the London winter. She was accompanied by her brother Edward, who drowned on 11 July 1840. *EBB/RH*, 5 October 1843, i, 162–3.

'*a very neat . . . I can be counted*': *EBB/RH*, 5 October 1843, i, 153. Horne writes 'herself' rather than 'myself'.

'*Writing . . . writing, writing . . .*': *EBB/RH*, 5 October 1843, i, 163.

Pan: god of shepherds and huntsmen: represented as having two small horns on his head, a flat nose, ruddy complexion, and a goat's legs and feet.

the potato disease in Ireland: the potato crop in Ireland had intermittently failed throughout the 1820s and 1830s. In September 1845 the first signs of widespread blight were reported and for the next two years the entire crop failed, leading to widespread famine, and the loss of 20 per cent of Ireland's population through emigration, disease, and starvation.

29 *Mrs Jameson*: Anna Brownell Jameson (1794–1860): writer, art historian, and social critic.

29 *'a very light complexion ... without breadth'*: EB to RH, 3 December 1844, *EBB/RH* ii, 167.

30 *Flush's co-operation*: EB to RB, 11 March 1846, *EB/RB* i, 549–50: 'he has been a very useful dog in his time (in the point of capacity), causing to disappear superogatory dinners and impossible breakfasts which, to do him justice, is a feat accomplished without an objection on his side, always.'

32 *'expressively'*: EB to H. S. Boyd, 22 June 1842, *EBBL* i, 107. '... he can't bear me to look into a glass, because he thinks there is a little brown dog inside every looking glass, and he is jealous of its being so close to *me*. He used to tremble and bark at it, but now he is *silently* jealous, and contents himself with squeezing close, close to me and kissing me expressively.'

33 *Flush 'is no hero'*: EB to Mr Westwood, August 1843, *EBBL* i, 149: 'Flush ... does not pretend to be a hero'.

over the bell-pull: EB to John Kenyon, *c.* December 1844, *EBBL* i, 224.

on her bed: EB to H. S. Boyd, 19 December 1843, *EBBL* i, 155.

'He is worth loving, is he not?': EB to RH, 5 October 1843, *EBB/RH* i, 166.

34 *early in January 1845*: RB's first letter to EB was postmarked 10 January 1845.

36 *'Do you think ... three months?'*: RB to EB, 12 March 1845, *EBRB* i, 41.

'April is coming ... Paracelsus ... a step and breath': EB to RB, 20 March 1845, *EBRB* i, 42–3. Paracelsus: Swiss doctor, alchemist and philosopher (1493–1541), hero of RB's dramatic poem of the same name (1835), who discovers on his deathbed the secret that had eluded him—that his great learning was inadequate without recognizing the knowledge that love brings.

44 *just as I did*: EB to RB, 9 July 1846, *EBRB* ii, 321. EB's apology begins: 'Ah Flush, Flush!—he did not hurt you really? You

will forgive him for me? The truth is that he hates all unpetticoated people, and that though he does not hate *you*, he has a certain distrust of you, which any outward sign, such as the umbrella, reawakens.'

'*expression of quite despair . . . having once known you?*': RB to EB, 10 July 1846, *EBRB* ii, 325.

'*no sooner . . . without a thought of it*': EB to RB, 13 July 1846, *EBRB*, ii, 329.

il se pose en victime: 'he made himself out to be a victim': EB to RB, 13 July 1846, *EBRB* ii, 329.

46 '*So he lay down . . . at me.*': EB to RB, 22 July 1846, *EBRB* ii, 353–4.

47 '*Wicked Flush . . . at least.*': ibid. 354. RB wrote to EB 23 July 1846 by way of reply: 'A "muzzle"? oh, no;—but suppose you have him removed next time, and perhaps the next, till the whole occurrence is out of his mind as the fly bite of last week—because, if he sees me and begins his barking and valiant snapping, and gets more and more heavier vengeance down-stairs, perhaps,—his transient suspicion of me will confirm itself into absolute dislike, hatred, whereas, after an interval, we can renew acquaintance on a better footing. Dogs have such memories!' *EBRB* ii, 357–8.

48 '*suddenly fell into a rapture . . . on the table*': EB to RB, 27 July 1846, *EBRB* ii, 363.

49 '*So I explained . . . goodness to him*': ibid. 363.

'*I need a week . . . a life!*': RB to EB, 12 July 1846, *EBRB* ii, 328.

50 *Vere Street*: just off Oxford Street, opposite New Bond Street.

12th of September: an error, but perhaps a significant confusion. EB's letter to RB telling him of Flush's kidnap was postmarked 2 September 1846: 12 September was in fact the date of the couple's marriage.

51 'This morning Arabel... do you understand?': EB to RB, 2
September 1846, *EBRB* ii, 505.

Mr Thomas Beames: (1814 or 1815–64), clergyman; author of
The Rookeries of London: Past, Present, and Prospective
(London: Thomas Bosworth, 1850).

52 'two in each seven feet of space': Beames, p. 167. The overcrowd-
ing figures come from a report drawn up by Mr Anselbrook, a
medical practitioner, addressed to the inhabitants of St James,
Westminster, 1847: they refer to cows.

53 'the most aristocratic parishes have their share': Beames, p. 24.

'wellnigh a penal settlement... in itself': Beames, p. 37.

54 'began to comfort me... at most': EB to RB, 2 September 1846,
EBRB ii, 506.

'smoking... with pictures': EB to RB, 3 September 1846,
EBRB ii, 510.

'doesn't know... I know perfectly': EB to RB, 3 September
1846, *EBRB* ii, 506.

58 'I must... bargain and haggle': EB to RB, 3 September 1846,
EBRB ii, 510.

60 'The archfiend... back with me': EB to RB, 4 September 1846,
EBRB ii, 515.

Mr Browning himself... never lose sight of...': RB to EB, 3
September 1846, *EBRB* ii, 513. Woolf significantly omits
what might have been noted, in RB's favour: that he was
writing to EB believing that now he had been located, Flush
must have been returned. He opens the paragraph: 'And now
that you probably have him by your side, I will tell you what I
should have done in such a case, because it explains our two
ways of seeing and meeting oppression lesser or greater' (ibid.
512).

61 '... it is horrible... have found out': RB to EB (postmarked 4
September, written 3 September afternoon), *EBRB* ii, 514.
He continues: 'But in this particular case, I ought to have told

you (unless you divined it, as you might) that I would give all I am ever to be worth in the world to get back your Flush for you—as your interest is not *mine*, any more than the lake is the river that goes to feed it,—mine is only made to feed yours—I am yours as we say—as I feel more and more every minute.'

'I think it lamentable weakness . . .': RB to EB, 4 September 1846, *EBRB* ii, 517.

Mr Barnard Gregory: (1796–1852), editor of *The Satirist* (1831–49) and *The Penny Satirist* (1837–46).

'But why write . . . in the world?': RB to EB, 4 September 1846, *EBRB* ii, 519.

to quote Donne: RB does not, in this part of their correspondence, appear to quote Donne; nor does EB reproach him for so doing.

62 *'But Flush . . . guilt in the world?'*: EB to RB, 4 September 1846, *EBRB* ii, 522.

'one word more . . . domineerers in general': RB to EB, 4 September 1846, *EBRB* ii, 520.

'Think of Flush': EB to RB, 4 September 1846, *EBRB* ii, 522.

'I am about to marry you': RB to EB, 4 September 1846, *EBRB* ii, 520.

63 *Manning Street, Shoreditch*: EB writes to RB, 6 September 1846, *EBRB* ii, 527, of 'Mr Taylor's in Manning Street, or Shoreditch [or] wherever it was.'

64 *'Out came . . . faces of those men!'*: EB to RB, 6 September 1846, *EBRB* ii, 526–7.

the most vivid passages in Aurora Leigh: see books III and IV of Elizabeth Barrett Browning's verse epic *Aurora Leigh* (1856), especially iv. 574–93:

> Faces! Oh my God,
> We call those, faces? men's and women's . . . ay,
> And children's;—babies, hanging like a rag

Forgotten on their mother's neck,—poor mouths,
Wiped clean of mother's milk by Mother's blow
Before they are taught her cursing. Faces? . . . phew,
We'll call them vices, festering to despairs,
Or sorrows, petrifying to vices: not
A finger-touch of God left whole on them,
All ruined, lost—the countenance worn out
As the garment, the will dissolute as the act,
The passions loose and draggling in the dirt
To trip a foot up at the first free step!
Those, faces? 'twas as if you had stirred up hell
To heave its lowest dreg-fiends uppermost
In fiery swirls of slime,—such strangled fronts,
Such obdurate jaws were thrown up constantly
To twit you with your race, corrupt your blood,
And grind to devilish colours all your dreams
Henceforth.

66 *'there seemed no other way . . . in good humour'*: EB to RB, 6
September 1846, *EBRB* ii, 527.

67 *'He was not . . . as I expected'*: EB to RB, 6 September 1846,
EBRB ii, 527.

71 *Hodgson's*: bookstore in Great Marylebone Street.

72 *dogs travel in boxes—followed*: EBB to Miss Mitford, 2 October
1846: 'I assure you that nearly as much attention has been paid
to Flush as to me from the beginning, so that he is perfectly
reconciled, and would be happy if the people at the railroads
were not barbarians, and immovable in their evil designs of
shutting him up in a box when we travel that way' (Percy
Lubbock, *Elizabeth Barrett Browning in her Letters* (London:
Smith, Elder & Co., 1906), 193–4).

Vaucluse: EBB to Mr Westwood, 10 March 1847: 'We made a
pilgrimage from Avignon to Vaucluse in right poetical duty,
and I and my husband sate upon two stones in the midst of the

fountain which in its dark prison of rocks flashes and roars and testifies to the memory of Petrarch.' *EBBL* i, 323.

74 *Pisa*: the Brownings were in Pisa from 14 October 1846–20 April 1847. After a few days in a hotel, they rented rooms in a sixteenth-century palazzo, the Collegio di Ferdinando.

the Kennel Club: organization founded 1873 which establishes dog breeds, records pedigrees, issues the rules for dog shows and trials, etc.

canaille: contemptuous term given to populace, rabble, mob. In the context of this book, it is a significant choice of words, since it comes from the Latin root *can-is*, with a collective suffix: literally, pack of dogs.

75 *Chatsworth*: principal seat of the Dukes of Devonshire, in Derbyshire.

'Flush has grown . . . rather like it': EBB to Mr Westwood, 10 March 1847, *EBBL* i, 323.

barouche landau: a barouche is a four-wheeled carriage with a half-head behind which can be raised or let down at pleasure, with a seat inside for the driver, and seats behind for two couples to sit facing one another. A landau is a very similar, though not identical, vehicle.

fly: a one-horse covered carriage—such as a cab or hansom—which is let out on hire.

76 *'in a blaze of undeniable glory'*: EBB to her sister Henrietta, 4, 5, 6 January 1848, *EBBS*, p. 69.

'struck back . . . the Venus': EBB to sister, 9 July 1847, *EBBS*, p. 39. Other letters to her sister contain further episodes relating to Flush which Woolf does not incorporate: on 16 May 1847 she records how Flush had suffered spasms, fits of screaming, and wouldn't touch water: they feared rabies, but he was cured by castor oil (*EBBS*, pp. 30–1); on 26 July 1853 she records how Flush was taken every morning to swim in the river: 'these baths are doing Flush an infinite deal of good already' (*EBBS*, p. 189).

76 *the Grand Ducal Court*: the court of the Grand Duke of Tuscany, the Austrian-born Leopold II.

77 *'It . . . English Court'*: EBB to sister, 4, 5, 6 January 1848, *EBBS*, p. 72.

Signor Righi: for Wilson's romance with Signor Righi, see EB to her sister, 19 November 1848, *EBBS*, pp. 94–8.

on to Florence: the Brownings stayed in five different sets of apartments in Florence: (i) furnished rooms in the via delle Belle Donne, from their arrival on 20 April 1847 to August; (ii) furnished rooms in the Palazzo Guidi for a couple of months; (iii) similar rooms in the via Maggio, taken for six months, but abandoned within ten days since they made EBB ill; (iv) furnished rooms in the Palazzo Pitti, for six months from early October 1847 to April 1848; (v) unfurnished rooms in the Palazzo Guidi, their 'Casa Guidi'.

'. . . he goes out every day . . . the little dogs': EBB to Miss Mitford, 5 November 1846, *EBBL* i, 307. She also wrote to Henrietta on 24 November 1846: 'If Arabel sees Flush in her dreams, he must disturb them—so impudent has he grown and noisy. It's his way of talking Italian': *EBBS*, p. 8.

Cascine: Florence's largest park.

'like emeralds . . . alive and flying': EBB to sister, 7 March–1 April 1848, *EBBS*, p. 80.

78 *'stands up . . . manner possible'*: EBB to sister, 10, 19, 20 February 1849, *EBBS*, p. 103.

'. . . he goes out . . . at his absence': EBB to sister, 10, 19, 20 February 1849, p. 103.

79 *'Quite disgraceful . . . like him'*: EBB to sister, 13 September 1847, *EBBS*, p. 47. EBB took a somewhat different view concerning the occasion of Flush's absence which provoked this remark, the huge demonstration recorded two paragraphs later: '. . . I don't doubt that the great crowd and confusion and illumination of the night before had frightened and confounded him, and that he had lost himself completely'.

EDITOR'S NOTES

scagliola: Italian plasterwork, designed to imitate kinds of stone.

such a shouting and trampling in the street: forty thousand people took part in a *festa*, filing under the windows of Casa Guidi, thanking Leopold II (1797–1870, ruled 1824–59). At first he continued the liberal reforms of his father Ferdinand III, and granted his people a constitution and a National Guard. This was short-lived: he was expelled by the revolutionary party and recanted his liberalism. See EBB to her sister, 13 September 1847, *EBBS*, pp. 43–6.

80 *'Viva Pio Nono'*: the Pope, born Giovanni Maria Mastai-Ferretti (1792–1878). He became Pope 1846, and immediately inaugurated liberal reforms in papal states and supported the cause of Italian nationalists.

'He confessed . . . long about it': EBB to Miss Mitford, 1 October 1847, *EBBL* i, 346.

81 *spotted spaniel*: EBB to Miss Mitford, 22 February 1848, *EBBL* i, 357.

'he had been very much amused': EBB to Miss Mitford, 1 October 1847, *EBBL* i, 347.

busy with her needle: 'Pen' (Robert Wiedemann Barrett Browning) was born 9 March 1849.

82 *Miss Blagden, Mr Landor, Hattie Hosmer, Mr Lytton*: Isabella (Isa) Blagden, writer and close friend of the Brownings, said to have been born in India, d. 1873; Walter Savage Landor (1775–1864), prose and verse writer; Harriet Goodhue Hosmer (1830–1908), popular American sculptor; Robert Bulwer Lytton (1831–91), poet and diplomat, son of Edward Bulwer Lytton, 'inclined to various sorts of spiritualism, and given to the magic arts', EBB to John Kenyon, 23 November 1852, *EBBL* ii, 97.

83 *'. . . for a whole fortnight . . . lavished on him'*: EBB to Miss Mitford, 30 April 1849, *EBBL* i, 402.

84 *'on the whole'*: EBB to Miss Mitford, *c*. July 1849, *EBBL* i, 412.

84 *Vallombrosa*: EBB to Miss Mitford, 20 August 1847: 'Flush hated Vallombrosa, and was frightened out of his wits by the pine forests. Flush likes civilized life, and the society of little dogs with turned-up tails, such as Florence abounds with.' *EBBL* i, 342.

85 '... *the exquisite ... preparing them*': EBB to Miss Mitford, 24 August 1848. *EBBL* i, 382–3.

86 '*Of these things ... any idea*': EBB to Miss Mitford, 24 August 1848, *EBBL* i, 382.

   Mr Swinburne: Algernon Charles Swinburne (1837–1909), poet, and supporter, like EBB, of Italian independence.

87 *Ruskin*: John Ruskin (1819–1900), art critic, and writer on social, economic, architectural, and environmental issues.

   George Eliot: (1819–80), novelist and literary figure. Her *Romola* (1863) is set in late fifteenth-century Florence.

88 '... *Savonarola's martyrdom ... in the summer*': EBB to Miss Mitford, 15 April 1848, *EBBL* i, 358. Girolamo Savonarola (1452–98), Dominican preacher, reformer, and martyr.

   for fleas: EBB to Miss Mitford, 20 August 1847, *EBBL* i, 342.

89 '*Robert is as fond ... as I am*': EBB to Miss Mitford, 2 October 1849, *EBBL* i, 424.

   '*wouldn't bear it ... likeness of a lion*': EBB to Miss Mitford, 2 October 1849, *EBBL* i, 424.

90 *Voltaire*: (François-Marie Arouet, 1694–1778), French writer and philosopher.

   '*Flush ... is wise.*': EBB to sister, 10, 19, 20 February, 1849: 'For wisdom, he gets wiser and wiser', *EBBS*, p. 103.

   the summer of 1852: Woolf is slightly confused here: EBB, RB, Pen, and Wilson left Casa Guidi to tour Northern Italy and Switzerland on their journey to England *c.*3 May 1851: they returned to Italy in the autumn of 1852.

91 *a lodging-house ... Welbeck Street*: Welbeck Street runs parallel with Wimpole Street.

92 *cholera*: there were major cholera epidemics in England in

1831–2, 1848–9, 1853–4, and 1866. See Huxley's comments in *EBBS*, p. 110.

Mrs Carlyle's dog Nero . . . suicide: in March 1850 Jane Carlyle's (1801–66) dog Nero jumped from a window in the Carlyle's Cheyne Row house, but cleared the area spikes and survived. See Thea Holme, *The Carlyles at Home* (London: OUP, 1965), 136–7.

93 *the Rev Charles Kingsley at Farnham*: see EBB to Mrs Martin, 2 September 1852, *EBBL* ii, 83.

Donatello's: Donatello (1386–1466), influential Italian sculptor of the early Renaissance.

94 *'. . . they seemed to me . . . and convenience'*: EBB to sister, 6 October 1851, *EBBS*, p. 141.

'Mr Carlyle!': Thomas Carlyle (1795–1881), essayist, historian, and biographer.

95 *'. . . he was ordered . . . poor dog'*: EBB to sister, 6 October 1851, *EBBS*, p. 141.

97 *the Countess of Blessington*: Marguerite Power Blessington (1789–1849), travel writer and novelist: EBB to Mrs Martin, summer 1852, *EBBL* ii, 79–80.

98 *Lord Stanhope*: Philip Henry Stanhope (1805–75), historian, and active in the public promotion of the arts. See EBB to Miss Mitford, 31 July 1852, *EBBL* ii, 79.

Mr Chorley: Henry Fothergill Chorley (1808–72), literary journalist. EBB to Miss Mitford, 31 July 1852, *EBBL* ii, 79.

Lord Stanley . . . at the facts: EBB to sister, 17 August 1855, *EBBS*, p. 221.

99 *'From the Legation to the English chemists . . . whist.'*: EBB to John Kenyon, 16 May 1853, *EBBL* ii, 117.

'expresses itself . . . alphabet': EBB to Miss Mitford, 15 July 1853, *EBBL* ii, 123.

'scoperte a Livorno': 'discovered at Livorno' (Leghorn): EBB to John Kenyon, 16 May 1853, *EBBL* ii, 117.

99 *'four hundred thousand . . . spiritual intercourse'*: EBB to sister, 6 November 1854, *EBBS*, p. 208.

Arthur Russell: (1825–92), politician and host to political and literary society.

'But . . . the marvellous.': EBB to Miss Mitford, 31 July 1852, *EBBL* ii, 79.

100 *Mr Frederick Tennyson and Mr Powers and M. Villari*: Frederick Tennyson (1807–98), brother of the Poet Laureate; Hiram Powers, sculptor (1805–73), settled in Florence 1837. EBB wrote a sonnet to his phenomenally popular statue, the 'Greek Slave'; Pasquale Villari (1827–1917), Italian historian, economist, and statesman.

'Florence dissolving . . . except Robert. . . .': EBB to Isa Blagden, 26 July 1853, *EBBL* ii, 125. She also describes RB's scepticism in a letter to her sister, 30 August 1853, *EBBS*, p. 194, commenting: 'There are differences in the degree of receptiveness in the physical organizations of men and women.' RB's poem 'Mr Sludge, "The Medium"' (1864, probably drafted 1859–60) satirizes spiritualism.

Mr Kirkup: Seymour Stocker Kirkup (1788–1880), artist and antiquarian with a strong interest in spiritualism and the occult.

'You know . . . get out': EBB to Miss Mitford, February 1853, *EBBL* ii, 102.

101 *'that Flush's hair may grow'*: EBB to sister, 4 March 1854, *EBBS*, p. 199.

102 *'also . . . as distinctly'*: EBB to sister, 17 August 1855, *EBBS*, p. 220. The letter makes no mention of Flush.

104 *'Matta! Matta!'*: 'Crazy! crazy!' ('matto', as the masculine form, would be correct here).

106 *perfectly still*: Flush died in the summer of 1854, which came as 'quite a shock' and 'a sadness' to EBB: see letter to her sister Arabel, 17, 18 June 1854, Henry W. and Albert A. Berg Collection, New York Public Library.

American Literature

British and Irish Literature

Children's Literature

Classics and Ancient Literature

Colonial Literature

Eastern Literature

European Literature

Gothic Literature

History

Medieval Literature

Oxford English Drama

Poetry

Philosophy

Politics

Religion

The Oxford Shakespeare

A complete list of Oxford World's Classics, including Authors in Context, Oxford English Drama, and the Oxford Shakespeare, is available in the UK from the Marketing Services Department, Oxford University Press, Great Clarendon Street, Oxford OX2 6DP, or visit the website at www.oup.com/uk/worldsclassics.

In the USA, visit www.oup.com/us/owc for a complete title list.

Oxford World's Classics are available from all good bookshops. In case of difficulty, customers in the UK should contact Oxford University Press Bookshop, 116 High Street, Oxford OX1 4BR.

D. H. LAWRENCE	The Rainbow
	Sons and Lovers
	The White Peacock
	Women in Love
	The Widowing of Mrs Holroyd and Other Plays
KATHERINE MANSFIELD	Selected Stories
VIRGINIA WOOLF	Between the Acts
	Flush
	Jacob's Room
	Mrs Dalloway
	Night and Day
	Orlando: A Biography
	A Room of One's Own and Three Guineas
	To the Lighthouse
	The Voyage Out
	The Waves
	The Years
W. B. YEATS	The Major Works